THE SONG OF THE SLEEPERS
A NOVELLA

THE REST TO THE GODS

JOSHUA WALKER

Praise for The Rest to the Gods

A stunning world that's just as ancient and lived-in as it is fantastical, and an emotional epic of perseverance in the face of overwhelming odds. Walker delivers you straight into an immersive experience that can't be put down.

Rob Leigh, Author of *Pathlighter*

A captivating story of courage and resilience, set in a beautiful world that is brilliantly realized. In The Rest to the Gods, *Walker has given us an appetizer that leaves you begging for dinner.*

Scott Palmer, Author of *A Memory of Song*

An illuminating story of tradition, self-worth, and the purpose of power.

David J Neumaier, from *David's Indie Book Review*

A gripping tale of sacrifice and belonging, layered amidst an imaginative setting full of wonder and peril.

Calum Lott, Author of *A Dirge for Cascius*

Josh Walker weaves poetic prose into a beautifully immersive world that will instantly pull you in.

Isaac Hill, Author of *The Dragon Rebellion*

BY JOSHUA WALKER

The Song of the Sleepers

Main series
An Exile of Water & Gold (Coming 2024)

Novellas
The Rest to the Gods

For my wife,
Because just like Nischia,
you are elegant, you are strong…
You are undefeatable.

CONTENTS

A note on the English language

Before you read The Rest to the Gods, I need to own up about something.

I'm Australian. Unabashedly so, right down to the very core of my grammatical expression. I **apologise** to everyone for this in advance.

As a result, please don't be concerned if you **realise** something is wrong, or think I've committed an **offence**.

If you can **manoeuvre** your way through the story without **pretence**, you might just enjoy it!

And don't worry – there are no **pyjamas** or **breathalysers** here, though there are some **travellers** to share the journey with.

Josh, the Australian grammar guy

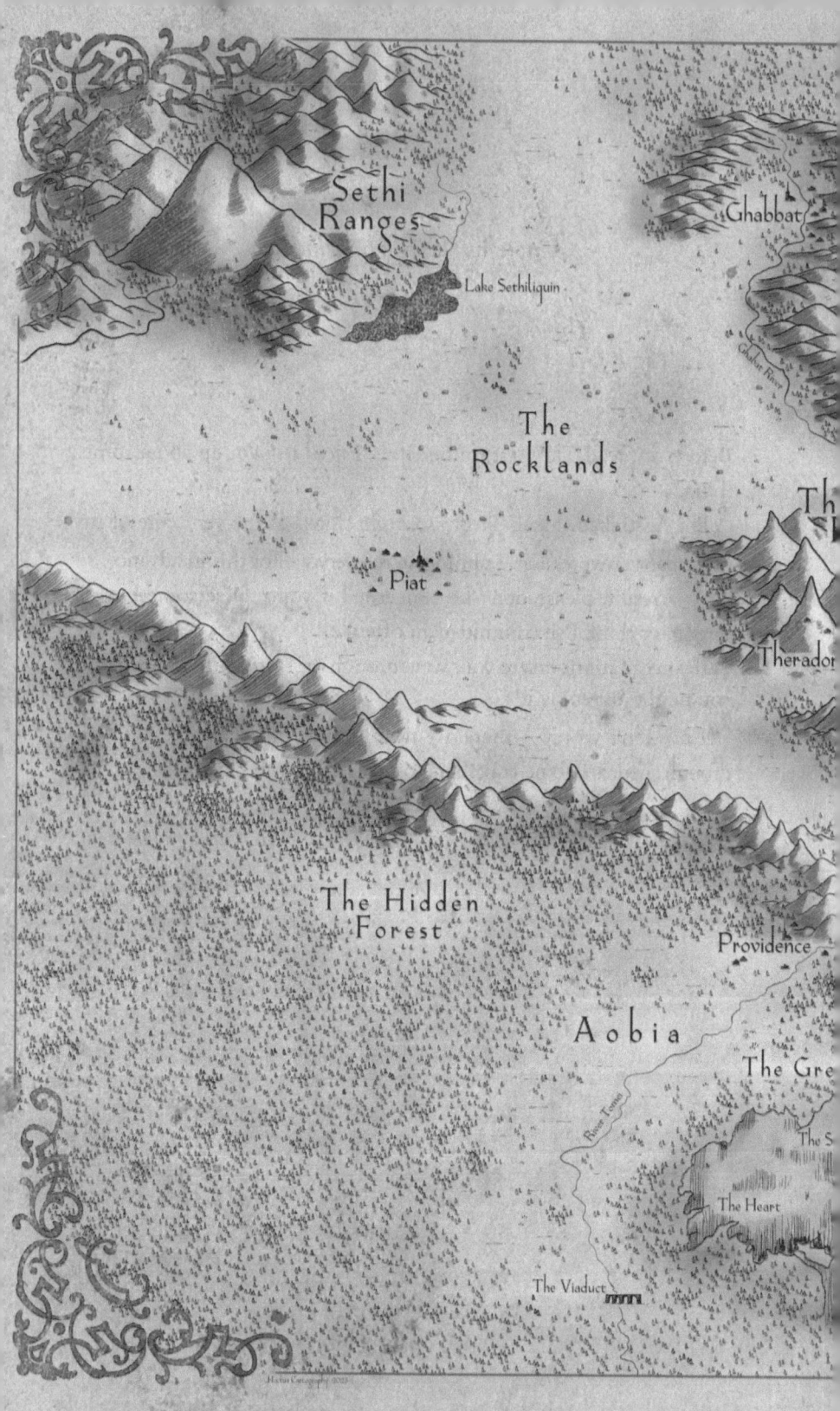

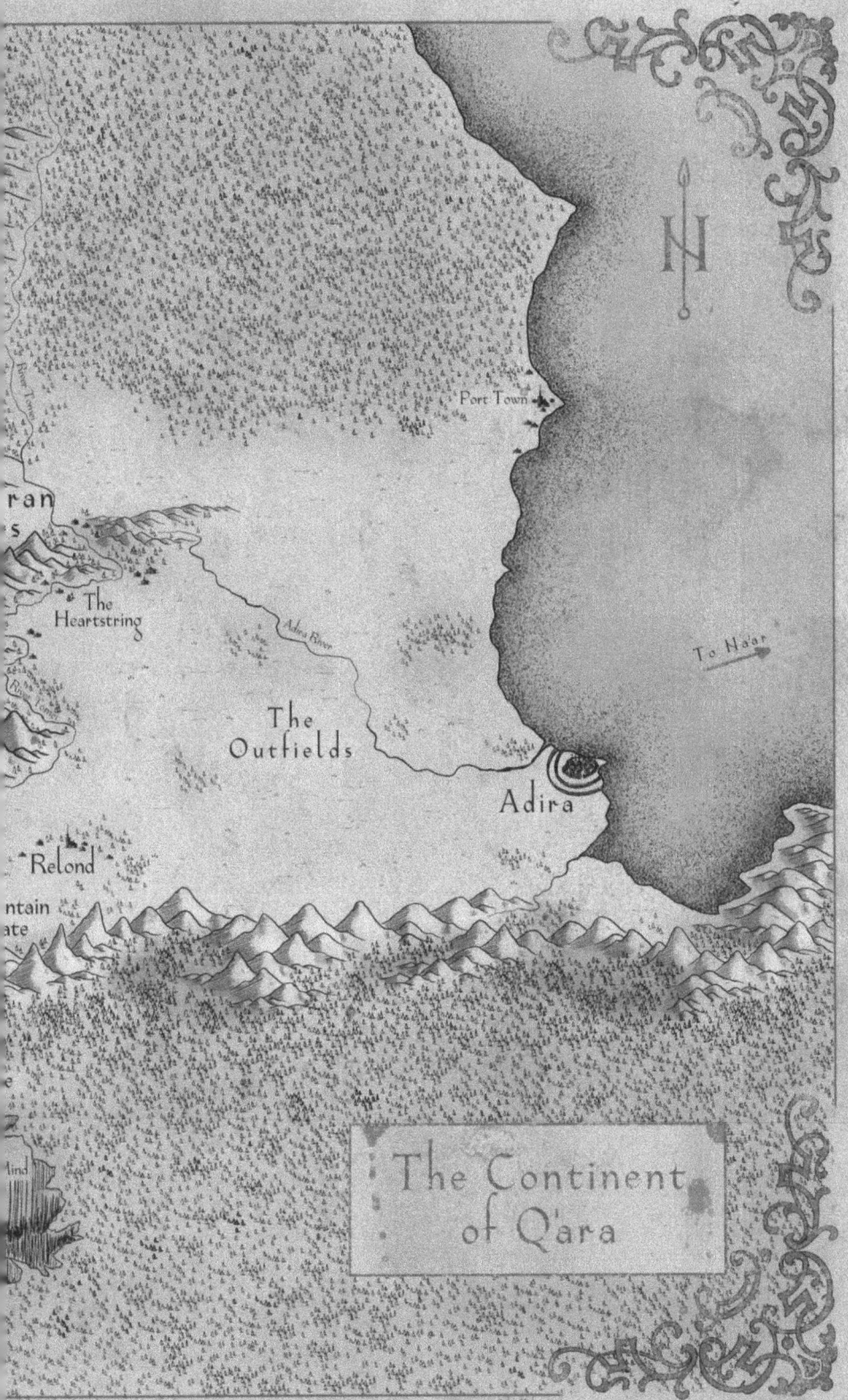

The Continent
of Q'ara

Do your duty, and leave the rest to the gods.

- Pierre Corneille, *Horace* (1639)

NOW

2055 AS (After Settlement)

CRUNCHING BONES.

Blood, dripping from spear tips, hammering down onto steel plate. The cries of another soul finally letting go of the material world.

This was the backdrop to every night's sleep since arriving at the Mountain Pass.

Tonight, the war raged on farther down the escarpment, in the direction of Therador, but Nischia was required to retire from the battlefield, and regenerate as quickly as possible. The demands were enough to cause sickness under any normal circumstance, but here, it was as though the adrenaline kept her trudging along. Her Orb lingered in the corner of her tent, and there she was untouchable.

She needed to Sleep, but first, she needed to sleep. There would be more *cism* to fill, empty and worthless until she was able to transfer any of her Luminosity to them. Without the small, glass orbs, the Sleepers could not bring a good enough amount of Luminosity to the battlefield.

At home, in the arms of the Tree, she could charge twenty or more in a single Sleep. But this far from Aobia, every second spent in focused Sleep was another second taken from her peak of energy. Another second where she might have slipped up, made an error, and died fighting, or worse.

After today, she felt weary, having used all the *cism* available to her and her team of twenty or so Sleepers to push the Theradoran line back from the peak of the Pass, where the land was wholly no man's. Such a tiny space, contested fiercely, causing the greatest bloodbath the continent of

Q'ara had seen in centuries. Sure, there may have been other battles in other places, all a part of the war effort, but here was the culmination of every nation's attempt to capture an essential territory.

She tossed in her bedroll, sighing. The mixed dissonance of the injured and dying bled through her tent walls like a fever dream, as though they were real, but could be heard in her mind all at once. Her people, whom she was sent to protect. Had she done enough? Had the precarious position of leadership moulded her into a better version of herself, or was she just a kind of demi-god for the common folk, an unreachable aspiration?

Three weeks, Nischia. Only three to go. They'd been on a rotating schedule of sorts, ever since the fight for the Mountain Pass had become the more pressing of turns in the war. Nischia had been sent second, each Sleeper given a month in total to keep the Aobian fighters safe, motivated, and on task.

She shivered as the freezing wind ripped through the tent, the air poking up and under it. They were not even at the peak, but the rocky terrain mixed with the occasional snow drops this high up on the Pass made for a climate unlike anything she'd ever experienced, and only heard about in stories. *Roots below!* she swore, giving in to the Mountain's cruel attempts to stop her resting.

Standing up quickly, she pulled her bedroll off the ground, swishing it around her like a cape, hugging it tight. She flinched in pain, glancing down at her bandaged wrist, where the slash of an unintending friendly spear had caught her earlier in the day. As was necessary for any Sleeper who sustained an injury, Nischia had been escorted from the battle immediately, and retired to her tent for the afternoon.

In the corner of the tent, the Orb called to her, singing in its curious way, an assortment of overtones and harmonies that sounded like the song for longing itself. This was her lot in life; that much she knew and had finally accepted. But it didn't make it any less hard to refuse the Orb's song, not in the least when she was tired, and her fortitude had been sapped once more, like a boulder accumulating snow as it runs downhill, no longer in control of its own momentum. Even more, she found it hard to refuse, and she knew the Orb would heal her wounds faster than any other aid.

She still found it difficult to experience the 'oneness' with her Orb that many other Sleepers had suggested was entirely normal. She found it harder, more so, to let go of her family, all these years later. Especially knowing the war was ongoing. What was to happen to them? She'd gotten word from her superior, Koln, that her younger sister, Rili, had been sent to the Adiran front, deep in the outfields that connected Adira to Therador via the small collection of unallied towns called the Heartstring, which swept throughout the hills and plains, all the way to Ghabbat in the far north of the continent. Even if anything had happened to her, Nischia would not know. All the begging she'd done to get Koln to find out news of her family was exhausted, and she could not ask again. That was the agreement. As a Sleeper, your family were the other Sleepers, and your direct dependents were the entire population of Aobia.

Before leaning into the golden Orb, her arm nearly entering into its shimmering, mirror-edge surface, the tent door scratched and flickered, and she stiffened, sensing someone was outside.

"Sister!" the voice came in a piercing whisper. "Are you up?"

Nischia pulled the knots binding the flap-door to the tent walls loose, as the warm glow of her Orb behind her illuminated two faces in the night. Prisma, a young Sleeper who had completed her studies with Nischia stood with a lamp in hand, looking anxious. Her silver-blonde hair was tucked behind her ears, and her gaze was heavy.

Beside her, and at about a quarter of her height, was Sergeant Cavtil, a stout and steady leader of the artillery squadron here on the front. He was also a Nestler of the Hidden Ones, a species with whom Nischia had little experience before coming to the Pass. His weasel-like appearance had been hard to grasp at first—as cute as a button, but as savage as the wildest of fighters when in battle.

As it had turned out, the slowness of the Adiran allies' response was outpaced fiercely by the allegiance of the Hidden Ones, who agreed to fight with Aobia in order to protect the expanse of dense forestry to the south of the Pass. They did not, however, wish to have their allegiance associated by extension with King Filens of Adira. The entire culture of the Hidden Ones was still unsure of humanity as much as it was nearly two thousand years prior.

"Good night, Sergeant," Nischia greeted him, inclining her head in a small bow. "What brings you here at this hour?"

"We must come inside," Cavtil said gruffly. "The front is changing." He scurried past her, followed by Prisma, who said nothing.

Cavtil eyed Nischia's Orb with a kind of caution she had come to expect from non-Sleepers, sitting away from it. Even the odd common Aobian who had visited her tent for one reason or another had appeared uncomfortable before the otherworldly Orb. Cavtil's beady, black eyes seemed to shrink even more before the glowing entity, and he scratched his whiskers with a paw nervously. "Do not think it any small thing for Cavtil to come here, a Sleeper's tent, in the night."

"I do not, Sergeant," Nischia said, understanding.

Hidden Ones were oddly dubious about anything they themselves hadn't encountered in their culture. The Orbs were a more confronting part of Aobia's ways than anything else, it seemed, and every Hidden One reacted the same way, as though they were silencing some animal instinct to run away from them.

On the battlefield, however, they were vicious, fighting with spears and crossbows, and moving at such a speed that even the Aobians were taken by surprise. Nischia was glad they fought on the same side.

"Nischia," Prisma said pressingly. "Therador has found a new flanking route. Our spies have seen several enemy soldiers taking a cliffside path into the far corners of our own camps. If they manage to weasel their way in, they could expose us to an attack from behind, as well as the front. We'd be spread too thin to retaliate."

Cavtil shot Prisma a dark look, clearing his throat. Prisma looked at him, unable to read his expression.

"Weasel?" Nischia offered, trying not to chuckle as her sister Sleeper covered her mouth, aghast.

"I'm so sorry, Sergeant!"

Cavtil put up a tame paw. "Think nothing of it."

"Sister, you said our spies near the peak have seen the enemy take this path around the mountain. Why can they not track them further?"

"They came back here first," Prisma said. "They said the way was not clear. For Therador to push a unit through, they will need to cut back the scrub and bush. From a higher vantage, it doesn't seem possible to see much until things are cleared."

A shiver ran down Nischia's neck. She was afraid this would happen. It had already been five weeks at the Pass, and Therador would be getting desperate. They were clinging on, awaiting their newest allies in the Sethi ranges to travel with the Piatic armies, and grow their numbers. That's what this fight was really about: holding firm on the Pass, and reducing their numbers before their reinforcements arrived, in a desperate attempt to scare them into retreat.

"What of Adira, and Ghabbat?" The Sea Kingdom had found its own allies in the far north Ghabbatians, as well as the smaller coastal city of Port Town. They were fighting equally as hard to stop Therador from breaching the northern aspect of the Mountain Pass, but their numbers were dwindling, and it was impossible to supplement their forces with new units as fast as they needed. The Great Tree of Aobia was at least a week's ride south.

"The Adirans are pushing hard, Lady Sleeper," Cavtil said. "But even they are slipping farther down the northern aspect of the Pass. At this rate, they will end up at the base of the mountain within the month. Ghabbat is a two-week journey from here, and their forces are arriving, already defeated by the travel, and unable to fight for their own survival. Besides, they have been intercepted at several points across the front at the Outfields. If Adira's lines cannot push Therador back towards their own land, the breach will be like floodwaters, bursting at the gates."

"Well," Nischia began, rubbing her searing wrist absently, "the first thing we must do is clearly remove the flanking path that Therador is exploring. How many of their own have been sent off on that command?"

"A couple hundred." Cavtil shrugged. "A light force. But they would not expect an ambush from us, so a light force is all that is needed for such a quest."

"Of course," Prisma agreed. "All they are tasked with is clearing a path. Once they've done so, they wouldn't even need to show themselves—they could go back and return with a larger force on their own time."

"Sergeant, is there a route you know of that runs in parallel with the path they are attempting to clear?" Nischia asked. She knew the chances were low; the density of bush and scrub, combined with the steepness of the mountain's cliffs in places made it immensely treacherous to even consider trekking down an unknown path. If scouts were waylaid by any of the potential variables that made the mountain as wild as it was, they might never make it back.

"There is a single cliff face running above the path, from what Cavtil can see on the maps, Lady Sleeper," the Nestler responded. "But nobody knows the truth of the maps—we can only guess at the shape of the land by judging it in the context of what is around it, especially without having traversed it ourselves."

"I understand the ambiguity of the landscape, Sergeant," Nischia said. "We may not be able to say that this cliff face runs the length of the path the Theradorans have carved already. Could we send a small company of artillery with scouts to get the job done?"

Cavtil shook his head firmly. "Lady Sleeper, that would be suicide. The cliffs are too exposed. The soldiers may be able to remain out of sight for a time, but Cavtil suspects that once the first shot is fired, they will be outnumbered by the enemy."

"What is the ratio?" Nischia pressed. "I need to know how large a force we could send, Sergeant."

Cavtil took a deep breath, his paws scampering beneath himself to stay upright on the slippery, tarpaulin ground. "Greater than ten to one, Lady Sleeper. Two hundred enemy soldiers taking the flank route may not sound like much. But Cavtil knows that even eight of our own would be hard pressed to fit along the cliffs above them. What will we do then?"

Nischia glanced at Prisma, who appeared empty of solutions, shrugging. "Let me think a moment, Sergeant," she said. Her eyes went to her Orb. She had not the energy to Sleep, and overexerting herself could lead to … worse problems. It was a risk, to be sure, but the Orb sung to her still, and she nodded to herself, as though accepting her fate.

"Luminosity," Nischia said.

Cavtil and Prisma both fixed their gaze on her, eyes wide with interest.

"I could … accompany a team of scouts and artillery. I understand no more than eight will work, including myself. But if I can have a few of the soldiers carry *cism*, then I can use Luminosity to drive the Theradorans off if the surprise attack does not come to fruition."

"Sister," Prisma insisted, "what if you are caught in the crossfire? You could die!"

Nischia looked again at her wrapped hand, the dregs of blood staining the bandage. "Prisma, what do we not accept as part of this fight but death? Am I not to live for my people?"

"Live, *yes*, but—"

"Well, it logically follows that if I must live for them, then it is an equal duty to die for them." Prisma went to speak again, but Nischia cut her off with a raised hand. "Prisma, this is the chance we have. Cavtil, is there no alternative way of thwarting the flankers?"

"Once on the cliff face," the Sergeant began carefully, "you will all be standing within metres of your deaths. There may be, however, another wide enough path below the flanking route that the enemy could take. Cavtil cannot guarantee that is the case, Lady Sleeper."

"Thank you, Cavtil," Nischia said. "Then it appears this is our greatest chance at holding the Mountain Pass. If that is the case, I will not shirk my duty. Please, allow me now to Sleep within my Orb. I will need all the Luminosity we can bring to this fight."

"My Lady Sleeper," Cavtil said, standing respectfully, paws crossed over his chest. "Cavtil is humbled by your ability to put aside your fears for such a task. May the gods of the Woodland go with you and yours."

"My duty is to my people, Cavtil. By extension, that is your people as well, and Adira. Let me do that, and your gods can do with the rest what they will." The closest thing to a god Nischia knew of was the Tree, but even that was not close enough in her heart. The pain of her vocation, thrown upon her like she was chained to her destiny, continued to sting, years after accepting her destiny as a Sleeper.

Cavtil nodded awkwardly and turned to go. "Cavtil will supply an additional unit of five Nestlers. Perhaps Burrowers would be better, but they are not Cavtil's men to give. However, an extra team of our size and ability will fit, and offer additional protection. Have them safeguard the *cism,* Lady Sleeper. They will guard them with their lives."

Prisma stepped up to her, seizing Nischia's hands in her own. "My sister," she began, her voice thick with fear. "I will … try my best, persevere to my last breath if I must, to look after our own on the front. But please return with your life. I fear I am only half of what our people need without you."

Nischia smiled. "Three more weeks, sister," she said. "Three more weeks until we leave this gods-forsaken mountainside, and the blood running down it. Then we can go home and do what we must for our people. The battlefield will be the problem of whoever the Magisterium sends next." She stole her unwounded hand from Prisma's grip and cupped her cheek. "You will find a way. Your strength precedes you, sister."

Prisma nodded, shaking. "Three more weeks," she whispered before following Cavtil silently out of the tent. The cold air sliced through it, the door flapping erratically, a symbol of what might come.

Nischia sighed, turning back to the Orb. She would not resist its song, though Koln might be disappointed in her for that. But he would not know. Here, this far from the tree, she did not have to shield her mind from him; the reach of Aobia was not so great as that. She reached her arm once more into the Orb, the other side of it glowing with a fierce resonance from within, feeling warm and inviting, yet terrifyingly tiring, too. This Sleep she was about to fall into was not the sleep of rest. Too much, and she might lose herself. The fear of becoming a Remnant Core was enough to stifle even the weakest-willed of the Sleepers.

Her whole body drifted through the shimmering partition of the Orb, which distinguished its barrier from the outside world. Then she sat, legs crossed, and felt the thrum, the rhythm of its beat synchronised with that of her own heart. The song rose in her, like a wave, and she exhaled deeply, letting it echo in the far chambers of her mind. The sweet warmth of the Orb reaching out to her, and stealing her away from the world, was both intoxicating and paralysing.

Her soul stepped away from the reality she was aware of moments before, and pushed her down, deep into the furthest oceans of Light that it could go.

THEN

1957 AS

THE FEVER CAME THAT night, quietly at first. Legs trembling, breath thinner than usual, Nischia thought it was just the onset of the winter. In the last few days, snow had started to fleck across the tops of the Great Canopy, blocking more sunlight, and lowering the temperature in the Tree. Her parents lay sleeping in their own bed, one thin wall separating the two rooms. In the corner, her sister Rili slept soundly, obnoxiously unperturbed.

She sat up, reaching for a clay cup of water beside her bed, though there was none. Her throat had gone so dry, it hurt like razors were scraping at it every time she swallowed. Her hands began to shake in time with her legs, and then the teeth chattering began. The Fever took children as young as infants and as old as adolescents, and it was not an illness to wag a finger at, not the kind that could simply go away. She would either receive the Blessing of a new life from the Tree, or she would perish.

Already, the Fever had taken her brother, Mosche, when he was but a babe. Their mother had been sick then, not physically like he was when he died, but in the head. Something was wrong, like a darkness coated every behaviour, every expression, every word she spoke. She was never the same again.

Father had taken to the wine, and not the kind that was reserved for the Day of Life, at the start of Spring, but the kind that lowly and bleak folk found their way into. These people wandered the darker depths of the Heart, where she and her family lived. She had seen them from her window, or out in the street herself on the odd occasion, at night. The kind that sat back, sank into corners and crevices like they were comforted by an armchair, and sipped away their sorrows, their ordeals … maybe even their basic thoughts.

Her father had been drinking again, tonight, and now, she would have to wake him, expose herself to his wrath. The delicacy of such a thing could never be grasped. Not even when she'd been sick with minor things in the past, or clammy with terror from a nightmare.

The same recurring nightmare had stuck with her, since she was quite young, and she had it again tonight, the precursor to her symptoms. Her father, leaving her in the middle of the road, and exiting the Tree, never to return. She was so wracked with sorrow, and yet her heart was conflicted by the nightmare too—it affected her so, even though she knew that it was a step closer to Mother finding happiness again. If he left.

She crept out of bed, the floorboards creaking lightly, and stepped across the barrier of the hallway, into her parents' room. They lay nearly as soundly as Rili, but this was not without reason: Father was passed out from drink, yet again; while Mother was probably fighting the purpose in existence, as she did every other day. It was normal to see Mother retire from the world before the sun set in summer, and just after at this time of year, when there was a gloominess that held the world by the throat, threatening to silence it for longer, should it protest at all.

No; Mother would not stir. She reached for her father's shoulder lightly, taking a deep breath. "Father," she whispered gently, prodding his arm.

He seemed to open a single eye first, with a kind of caution that only crossed a person's face when they were between the world of dreams and the material kind. Then he snatched her by the arm, roughly, pulling her into the crook of his arm. "You threaten my family, wraith?" he hissed, teeth gritted. "What say you?"

Nischia struggled against his weight, trying to suppress a choking cough. "Father! It's me!" she cried, tears forming at the corners of her eyes as her body went limp, the air exiting her chest. She was already sick enough. Didn't he see her? Didn't he understand?

The floor rushed up to meet her face as Father flung her down, petrified at his innate reaction.

"My child." His voice broke. "I'm sorry."

She knew, as she always did, that he meant these words. But a genuine apology was not able to yield a change in his response before the next time. Her father was fixed, in all his flaws and talents.

"Father," she croaked, noticing her mother's body begin to stir behind them. "I am sick." Thrust out before him, her arms rattled, as though someone else was moving them against her will. Her teeth continued to chatter, and she found it harder to speak. Her body felt so hot, and yet so cold.

A horrified look crossed her father's face, as he edged toward her, gently taking up her arms. "My daughter," he sobbed. "What is wrong? Why are you trembling?"

Nischia felt her eyes flutter, and then roll back, the only thing in her vision the dim orange of her eyelids, and the world began to spin. A dull pain radiated from behind her skull, and the force of the spinning sent her to the ground, unable to manage her fall.

She tasted blood, and heard her father crying out, as her mother leapt up, screaming. She had bit down on her tongue and could not feel it properly. The world began to slip away, the sound of her frenzied parents becoming an echo in a chamber of darkness. Resigning herself to it, Nischia was at once removed from the world completely.

THE WALLS WERE WHITE when she woke; white and clean. Sheer curtains swayed in the midday breeze, as light sought its way through the room, like leaking water from a broken bucket. Voices could be heard uttering around her, barely above whispers, though they carried with them bustling energy. When she looked straight up, she noticed the decorated ceilings, embossed with the outline of flowers. Not just that—they were incredibly high.

This was not her home, she realised, and she began to panic. "Father," she started. "Father! Mama!" As her voice rose to its crescendo, violent and desperate, an equally desperate set of hands appeared before her, holding her down into the soft mattress upon which she lay. "No!" she screamed. "Get off me!"

"Stay still, child!" came the commanding voice. The head that the voice belonged to was completely concealed behind long waves of silver hair, wiggling around as the person tried to contain Nischia's outburst. "Koln? Koln, get over here! I need help. And *you*," the voice warned. "Stay still!"

Another set of hands came over, thrusting themselves upon her kicking legs, keeping them clamped down, and slowly, Nischia relented. When she stopped, she took in the newly revealed faces who were there by her bedside, and her heart dropped. She knew none of them. The first, a seemingly ageless lady with the silver, wavy hair, panting as she loosened her grip on Nischia's shoulders. The second was a male, stern looking, but much older, his hair a more peppery silver. An odd, yellow glow hung about them both.

A third person also appeared, in a bleach-white gown, tight-fitting gloves over her hands. She was young, and wore her blonde hair tied up behind her. Nischia recognised her clothing. A nurse. Was she in the Hospice at the Heart?

"No, child," the silver-haired lady whispered gently. "You're not in the Heart."

Nischia clambered back in her bed, sitting up startled. "How do you … ?" The lady had known her exact thoughts, as she thought them.

"Quiet, child," the lady said. "You're safe now, and there is ample time for explanations. Please, rest, change, and eat first. All the rest will come in good time." She nodded to the younger one who stood by Nischia's other side in her nurse-gown. "Lesse, would you fetch the girl some food? She hasn't eaten in days, and her stomach will be clawing at itself by now."

The nurse called Lesse nodded and darted off immediately, leaving Nischia alone with the two older strangers. "Who are you?" she asked.

The male replied, "The question, I think, is who are *you?*"

Nischia stared back at them blankly, feeling overwhelmed. She just needed answers. The desperation pulled at the fibres of her being. "I ... " Her throat caught, and her mind flashed back to the last thing she remembered. The clammy sensation all over her skin, the Fever, her father screaming at her ... The seizure. She shuddered.

"This child is not who we thought would take to the Blessing," the male uttered to his companion.

"No," she murmured in return. "Though we have gotten it wrong before."

"B—Blessing?" Nischia stammered, shaking her head. "I was so ill. So suddenly ill."

"Well, you are positively radiant now," the female said with a kindly voice, her outline glowing a resonant gold. "Take your hair in your hands and look."

Nischia sucked in a breath. She held up a tuft of fine, once-silver curly hair, where there lay now about it the same yellow glow that enveloped the two strangers at her side.

"You are a Sleeper, Nischia," the lady said gently.

The male continued to watch her with studious eyes, biting his thumbnail. "And you are to be apprenticed to me."

The lady shot him a glare. "This is Koln, Nischia. He will be your superior."

Koln grunted and turned his back on them, walking over to the nearby window. "Your parents do not wish to know of your whereabouts, child."

That caught her off guard. She didn't even have it in her to ask why, or to retort back at him.

The other Sleeper looked at Koln with scorn, like she wanted to slap him across the face. He balked, keeping his eyes off Nischia completely. An awkward moment passed, but Nischia could only feel the sting that was her broken heart.

Finally, she piped up over the incoming tears, "I want to be alone."

No questions, which deserved no answers. She knew all she had to. She just needed to fight through it. Her father must've known the sickness was the start of a Blessing, that she would be taken from them. Or maybe ...

She held back the tears for a brief moment, to no avail.

Maybe he wanted her gone *before* she was lost to them, just like her brother.

The two Sleepers left her in peace, Koln striding out of the room without a word, the other one, whose name Nischia still did not know, smiling morosely at her as she left, her dress whirling past, the air it caused in its wake rippling against Nischia's face.

In the quiet of the darkening day, edging closer towards the early evening of the winter, Nischia cried herself to sleep in a Hospice bed, alone. Abandoned.

Unbelonging.

THE RECKONING CAME IN the form of the new day's first break of the sun. Nischia woke to the light of the dawn, her eyelids grinding together the evidence of a disturbed sleep. She felt more rested, however, than she had in days, since the Fever had taken her. She felt ... alive, and sat, lost in the visage of her new self, and the aura of yellow that hung about her whole frame. If she could suppress what had happened to her in the past few days, if she could put aside what she knew her parents had done, casting her out without even a hint they cared about her whereabouts and safety—maybe then, she could find her way again.

But what about her life could she forget so quickly, so easily? What about her sister, Rili? Nischia was certain her younger sibling was terrified, both of what had happened to her, and the life Rili now faced, the only child of two broken parents.

"We can make her forget you, if it's easier," came the voice suddenly, interjecting in Nischia's thoughts.

"Please stop!" Nischia growled. She would not be toyed with. "You've done enough. I am already nothing—how much less than myself should I feel?" She sniffed. *No, Nischia,* she told herself. *Not tears again. You are harder than steel now. You* must *be.*

The Sleeper who had seen her the day before sat down on her bed. "I see much of myself in you, child," she said, intrigue lighting up her face. "I am Feldra." She offered Nischia a hand, which she gripped begrudgingly.

"Feldra," Nischia said beneath her breath, her nod slowing as realisation took hold of her. She gasped. "My queen!" Nischia bowed her head low, putting a pious forehead to the older Sleeper's arm.

"After four hundred years," Feldra said, somewhat ungraciously pushing away, "I am still not at ease with that title. I do not believe Aobia is her best self with a queen at the helm. Why not just be a people, a wave of innovation, of love, and culture? It saddens me that my rulership is the more logical option to our people. Not a day of my life have I thought it anything but folly."

The queen of Aobia was sitting here, on the edge of *Nischia's bed!* Who was she to deserve such a visitation? Why couldn't she have been more grateful yesterday when she woke to Feldra standing over her?

"My queen, I am so sorry!" Nischia said, mortified at her own ignorance. She should have wondered who this supposedly high-ranking Sleeper was when she first saw her.

"Nothing of the sort," Feldra said, dismissing her apology with the brush of a hand. "I am sorry for what you have endured, child. The Sickness, it … holds tight, like glue. I know it. I will never forget the feeling." The queen seemed to shudder at the thought, and a frown deepened across her forehead.

"My family," Nischia said quietly. "Is what that Sleeper said yesterday true?"

Feldra suppressed a chuckle. "*That Sleeper* is your superior now, Nischia. And he has a name."

"I'm sorry," Nischia apologised again, looking down at her bedraggled sheets. "It's just that he spoke without awareness that his words might have hurt to hear. And they did."

Feldra raised an inquisitive eyebrow, her mouth dropping, slightly aghast. "Child, you must not speak this way in Koln's presence. You've survived the Sickness—be sure not to ruin your chances of surviving thereafter with your words. Perhaps you two are not so different after all, and I can be at ease knowing I apprenticed you to him."

Nischia clenched her jaw with dissatisfaction. So, she would be studying under Koln, the tactless, stern Sleeper she had met the day before. Who didn't flinch or bat an eye when he told her that her family wanted nothing to do with her. She was an outcast now, a child without a true home, and he had told her all about it like a historical fact he'd read in a book.

"You will find the next few years difficult, child," Feldra said, breaking the string of Nischia's thoughts.

"What am I to do?" Nischia asked, sarcastic. "I have no choice otherwise."

"True." Feldra nodded. "But what you will learn will change you, the core of who you are, forever. Do not think that by hardening your heart you can accomplish your every goal in this life, child."

"What is it to be a Sleeper, besides lighting the streets and living in recluse, away from your people?" Nischia knew the words were harsh, and she intended them to sting every step of the way they made into Feldra's ears.

"I am a patient person, child," Feldra said. "But the Blessing that has been bestowed upon you is no small charge. The Tree in which we live

... There is a reason we call its strongest limbs our provinces: Heart, Mind, and Soul. It is a part of us, as much as we are it. Whether you are a Sleeper or not makes no difference."

Nischia got up from her bed and wandered over to the window, looking out at the orange microleaves that dotted the roadside and the roofs of other buildings. The Great Tree, retiring somewhat for hibernation.

"You speak like we are all equal, my queen," she said. "But you act, as do all your kind, like you are a god."

Nischia felt the drive of the queen's gaze in her back. "Not a god, Nischia. We are not the ones who gave our people the Tree to live in." She stood up and joined Nischia at the window, standing with the majesty owed to her, the title she had been given clear as the day. "I am just an Aobian with a Blessing, and with that Blessing comes a duty. An honour. The rest is for the gods."

NOW

2055 AS

NISCHIA HEARD THE SOUNDS of the world around her return as the light of daybreak broke her from Sleep. Hours before, she had been so far down the depths of her Orb, nothing could break the connection, but the Luminosity she felt flowing through her had reached a point where nothing new could remain, like air, locked between a bucket and water.

The rushing sensation of time returning to normal felt like an avalanche, racing to smash her in her stride, and her eyelids shuttered open as she gasped, pushing out of the Orb. Reverberating sounds filled her ears, and she took a moment to calibrate herself against reality, steadying her feet as she stood up.

As she looked ahead to her tent flap, Prisma stepped in from the morning chaos of soldiers rising, eating, and preparing to fight. The sounds of the sick and dying had quietened for now, as they usually did in the morning. Right now, it was a suicide mission up on the Peak. Nischia knew that. It was no different for any other army, either. But if she could ruin Therador's attempt at a flank, it might weaken them enough for Adira to push hard from the other direction and send them into a forced retreat. If the battle at the Mountain Pass ended, the Great War itself would have what it needed to follow in its steps.

"Sister, sorry!" Prisma said, averting her gaze as though she'd stepped in on Nischia naked. She hauled in a cart behind her, filled with dead, grey *cism*, ready to be charged with Nischia's fresh intake of Luminosity. "I was coming over to wake you from Sleep."

"It is okay, Prisma," Nischia said, corralling her thoughts. "I just returned, so I'm … not yet with it."

"You need to eat," Prisma said hurriedly. "Let me go and get you someth—"

"No," Nischia interrupted. "I can make do. Tell me, do you have the soldiers gathered?" She began to press her hands to each of the dead *cism* in the cart, new light blooming in the centres of the small, glass spheres.

Prisma nodded, folding her arms. "Ours, yes. Cavtil is yet to return with his own Nestlers, like he promised, though I'm sure he won't be far away." The camp they shared with the Hidden Ones was extensive enough as it was; finding one's way around it was akin to finding a snowflake amongst the Pass's own whitecap.

"All right. Show me who we've got," Nischia nodded stiffly, aware that she was still slightly dizzy as she finished filling the *cism*. There would be no way to Sleep in her Orb again until this mission was over. These *cism* would be all she had.

Stepping out into the camp brought with it a rush of icy wind. She'd had the privilege to travel over the Mountain Pass time and time again these past few years, but she never adjusted to its climate, especially not living beneath the cooling, temperate cover of the Great Canopies in Aobia. Even the snow at home didn't seem to bite as much. She glanced out over the edge of the mountain. The visibility was so high that she could see the Tree all the way from where she stood. Her heart ached.

Before her shaking self, a row of seven able-bodied soldiers stared at her, grim expressions dawning across their faces. They all wore signature green cloaks around their armour, fastened together with a silver brooch, the image of the Great Tree.

The sun was overcast today, and there seemed no chance of it poking out from amongst the dense clouds. At the front of the line was a male Aobian, tousled silver hair cut to shoulder length, and tied off at the end. A thick, but short beard covered his entire jaw and cheeks. "My Lady Sleeper," he said, bowing. "I am Arondil, commander for the thirty-first."

Thirty-first? So, this was what she was being offered for the job. The last unit off the rank yet to fight. "Artillery?" she asked, demure.

Arondil shuffled uncomfortably in his place. "Y-yes, my Lady Sleeper."

"You can call me Nischia," she said, extending a hand. "And there are more of you …?"

"There are, my—Lady Nischia," Arondil said, struggling with the name change. "However, I appointed my auxiliary commander this morning as soon as we rose and picked the five best I have to offer you. We are to run a flanking route around the Peak?"

Nischia ignored his question, frowning at the numbers before her. "Five? You are coming with us, Commander?"

Arondil did not sway. "I am, Lady Nischia."

"Hm." She looked him up and down. He was certainly of the right frame and build, as were most artillery fighters—nimble enough to move quickly with the lighter weight of a bow, and fast enough to spring into position as needed. Arondil also had a staggeringly chiselled jawline, the angle of which seemed to send some kind of shiver down Nischia's spine when she noticed it.

"I fear there will be bloodshed, Commander." She said it matter-of-factly, hoping her words would cast the other soldiers' eyes down in reconsideration. She had to be sure the people Arondil had picked knew what they were getting into.

It was no small thing, to run in the face of the enemy, at less than one-tenth the numbers. When she, Prisma, and Cavtil had agreed this would be a suicide mission, there was not a moment of any other possibility crossing her mind.

"We have been informed by Lady Prisma of the circumstances," another soldier said, stepping forward. The young female set steel-hard eyes on Nischia, with such a determination that her gaze seemed stronger than the gusts that pushed on them all constantly.

"Tersa," Arondil bit in warning. "Know your place."

"Your name," Nischia said, interjecting. "Tersa? How very fitting, child." She smirked, watching the young lady's nostrils flare. That kind of bull-headed pride would get them killed. But it could also save them. She would have to watch the young one with careful eyes.

Tersa bit her lip but did not speak again.

Arondil edged forward uncomfortably. "Lady Nischia, we are all a fierce bunch, though undoubtedly, we cannot prove it, as we've never been posted on the Peak. The bloodshed there hurts more deeply day by day. Whatever we can do to aid the war effort, we will do. We place ourselves entirely in your hands."

"You're a patriot, Commander?" Nischia mused. "I'd wager there aren't many of those left in Aobia. Not these days." Not since Feldra. She skipped over the thought. It stung nearly as much as memories of her family, repressed as they were.

"Not a patriot, Lady Nischia." Arondil shook his head seriously. "I think I speak for us all when I say that we just want to do some good here. What we believe in matters little when all we wish for is peace."

"Good," Nischia murmured. "Come, introduce yourselves. I may be a Sleeper, but I am not untouchable. I am Aobian, like the rest of us."

Arondil stepped back, gesturing for Tersa to also move aside. Another male, broader in the shoulders than Arondil, and more brooding, stepped forward, but struggled to keep eye contact with her. Nischia didn't know whether that was a product of her societal place, or something of his character, until he spoke softly.

"I am Hadi, my lady," he said, barely above a whisper, so that his words were nearly one with the wind. "I come from the Heart, a Branchrender's son."

Nischia smiled warmly at him. "A Branchrender's son. A noble lineage. Aobia would have a lot less without your father's kind." Branchrenders were those who twisted parts of the Great Tree into homes, buildings, and other infrastructures. They rarely cut into the Tree but would often construct things from dead limbs collected over the winter, from higher up in the Canopies. Their work was as dangerous as it was necessary.

Hadi bowed his head in acknowledgement, stepping back. Next was Wes, a supply-officer who shared equal responsibility for the ammunition reserves with Freya, a quiet but stern looking one. Beside them were Valton and Gest, twins who had come from the Soul, their family a long line of needleworkers. They were the trackers who would be leading the group on their venture, and hopefully predicting when conditions changed, well ahead of having to face them.

"We are ready for your command, my lady," Arondil said when they had finished exchanging their introductions. "We make no exceptions for ourselves."

Nischia stifled a laugh. "I'm glad to hear it," she replied drily. "But we have another set of tasks ahead of us before we leave, one of which is that we make as accurate a topography as we can based on how we surmise the side of the mountain to be. Trackers, can you stay ahead of us the whole way?"

Valton and Gest both nodded eagerly. "We can, my lady," Gest said, her green eyes vivid against the flat white backdrop of the snow, which had again begun to fall in a light patter. "We'll leave right away; we have everything with us."

"Thank you," Nischia said. "I know what you survey will not be an accurate representation of the paths we are to walk, but anything we can take with us is useful against an unknown set of variables like those we are dealing with."

"And the enemy?" Arondil said, eyebrows raised with worry. He looked protectively at his trackers, averting his gaze as soon as Nischia caught on.

"The enemy is reportedly travelling in numbers twenty times our size and could make quite a dent in our reinforcements if they make it through to this side of the Pass."

"Canopies …" Tersa breathed, cupping a fretful hand to her mouth. "A dent?"

"It is always better to underpromise, and overdeliver," Nischia said. "But I will not dally around the matter for any longer: the risk of having the enemy penetrate our lines in our own encampment could shift the entire course of this battle, and the repercussions of that, I fear, will be felt far from this Mountain, let alone this side of the Continent." Silence covered the group like the snow, but Nischia went on. "Luckily, I have the word of our greatest allies that we can maximise our numbers, to a tenth the size of the enemy's infiltrators."

"I was told we would not fit more than eight in total," Arondil stated.

"And you would be correct," Nischia said, pursing her lips. "If we were talking about Aobians, that is. The Hidden Ones will provide us with an additional group of five Nestlers, to support in their nimble ways—carrying goods and supplies and using the smaller spaces along the path wherever the need arises. Keep them out of sight, and they may just be the trump card we need when we inevitably hit the enemy lines."

At that moment, the group turned to see Sergeant Cavtil arriving, accompanied by the promised Nestlers, who were trudging through the snow behind him. "Lady Nischia." He nodded as he approached.

Nischia smiled back politely. "General, we are much obliged. Thank you for bringing your soldiers to assist us."

Cavtil shook his head. "Cavtil should be the one saying he is obliged, Lady Nischia. If this army breaches our side of the mountain, it will begin the turning point Therador needs to gain the upper hand in this battle." He gestured to his team of Nestlers, gathered stoically behind him. "Nobody wants to drag this battle out any longer than it has gone on already. These are five of Cavtil's fiercest Nestlers. Cavtil recommends you use them for supply carrying, and perhaps to work with your own trackers as you walk the unknown path before you."

Nischia smiled as the Nestlers disbanded, forming a neat line so that they could introduce themselves, one by one to her. She loved these people. The Hidden Ones embraced a kindness beyond kindred—every person met by them was greeted with the utmost politeness, and a friendly paw, raised in the air as a greeting.

Nischia raised a hand back at each one as they passed her, trying to memorise their names, though the similarity in Hidden One names continued to prove a difficult thing to navigate with her mind. Arv, Riv, Scov, Bvil, and Garv were their names, and though she managed to bank them all, she knew she would not be able to tell them apart in the time they would be sharing together. Then again, that was not her job; to succeed in this mission meant to work as one, with care, no matter the costs.

"Welcome, Nestlers of the Hidden Forest," she said formally. "My own Aobian soldiers, and I, cannot express our gratitude enough that you will be joining us."

Cavtil harrumphed behind her, interjecting. "The trackers you have chosen, who are they?" Valton and Gest raised their hands at the same time. Cavtil peered at them, as though evaluating their worth. "Arv and Riv will assist you, tree-dwellers. They are our finest scavengers and path cutters. Even those of us who fight on the Peak right now do not have accompaniments as talented as they." He smoothed out his whiskers so that they curled up neatly around his pointed nose. "Scov and Bvil are your quarter-fielders. They can cook a meal worth more than your talents combined, as well as lug supplies in formation. Keep them hidden, and behind your main line. Cavtil will now let Commander Garv introduce himself."

The Nestler known as Garv was older in his years than the rest of them, possibly including Cavtil himself. Garv's hair was greyer, and blacker, and it seemed more uneven and matted in places than the younger Nestlers. The most noticeable thing about him, however, was his face: above his snout was one well-seeing eye, the other having been replaced at some point with a fierce looking scar, as though the skin had been folded in to close the hole that used to be there.

"Commander Garv is at your service," he said with a low, growl-like voice, not dissimilar to the crunch of stones underfoot. "We fight with you, tree-dwellers. We are faster and nimbler on foot than you Aobians, who are as tall as our own trees, and we make less errors than the pathetic humans Therador seems to be known for."

This older Nestler was weathered, and Nischia believed he had seen significant turbulence in his life, judging from his tone and energy alone. Garv seemed to let his head down more than the others, like he'd been alive long enough for even that to sap his energy. His tail was nearly hairless, compared with the bushy, long tails of his companions. But he was respected, and Cavtil seemed to edge away when he spoke, as though his shadow was longer than the rest of the Nestlers.

"Commander, I am indebted to you for aiding us on this mission," Nischia said, raising her hand once more in the customary greeting of the Hidden Ones. "The forest we share is great, made so by our two people and the stewardship we take of it. I have faith that this same collaboration of our peoples will secure us the outcome we are hoping for in the coming days."

Garv took a moment to eye her up and down, slowly but surely. Nobody made a sound. Eventually, he snorted a low, but somewhat agreeable snort, and shook himself so that the flecks of snow that were filling in the gaps between his fur spat out into the wind. He resumed his place among the other Nestlers and said nothing more.

"Cavtil, we must leave soon," Nischia said. "I'd like to be on the track before nightfall."

"Of course," Cavtil replied. "The enemy will not have progressed much today in this snow. Let us set off immediately—Cavtil and Prisma can show you the path we surveyed yesterday."

The war camp was no small allotment for the mountainside, stretching a good half league or so across an open field that sat a hundred metres or so lower than the Mountain Pass peak, which overhung them in the distance like a reminder that they lived in the shadow of war, day in and day out.

The camp had originally been segmented into a great number of areas, firstly by units, then ranks, and then additional services, such as the Hospice that Prisma had worked on in their first days on the mountain. That Hospice had now quadrupled in size, Nischia noted as they marched through the camp, having swallowed up the various units' spaces as the battle had waged on.

Now, regular living spaces for soldiers who were waiting for deployment, or coming back into the fold, had been replaced, filled with anguished bodies searching for warmth, repair, or simply a quieter place to die.

"I fear things are getting far more desperate than we had planned for, sister," Nischia said in a low voice to Prisma, who walked beside her.

"When you get back, things might be very different," Prisma agreed.

Nischia sucked in a loud breath. "Things *will* be, and not in our favour either, if I can't manage to suppress the flanking force."

Prisma stopped there, in the field. Beside her, a Sleeper nursed a quietly dying footman, who had taken a nasty slash in the side. How he'd made it back to the camp, Nischia would never know. Prisma reached out, gripping her wrist. "You'll find a way, sister. You out of all of us, always find a way. The talk of armistice grows only louder by the day. We just need to hold fast."

"We shall see," Nischia said. "Just like the first day I found out my fate, sister, I have been spoken of more highly than the results I feel I am capable of producing. I know it is not your intention, but I live with the expectations of everyone around me, like a boulder, slowly weighing me down, picking up more mass the longer I try to hold it up." She felt glassy-eyed and sniffed lightly. "If I am to fail, I ask you now to forgive me."

Prisma said nothing, returning only a sad smile. The moment was broken when Commander Arondil interrupted with a loud clearing of his throat. "We are not far from the boundary of the camp, Lady Sleepers," he said. "I will march the rest of us forward to General Cavtil, so that he might point out the way we are taking. Valton and Gest have already begun their own walk."

He nodded stiffly and moved away from them. His chiselled jaw seemed to hold high in the morning sunlight, and his peppery hair swung back casually over his ears, immovable in the face of the wind.

Prisma sighed, disrupting Nischia's thoughts. "We must go, sister. Please—do not think of yourself in such ways. You are an inspiration to me, and many others. Forgiveness does not even feature in the matter."

Nischia blushed lightly, but they continued on behind the trail of fifteen Aobian and Nestler fighters. They were coming to the beginning of the mission, the start of a nearly impossible plan to execute. Deep down, Nischia knew she would be forgiven.

But equally, she knew that if they failed, she would not forgive herself. That was her curse.

THEN

1957 AS

THE ORB FIRST APPEARED as a mirage, an oasis in the desert of her fever. Nischia had seen glimpses of it when she was in the depths of her sickness. In the darkest hours of the night, it had come to her like a saving light, a replenishing fill that she could not take.

Aobians had never been desert people, but she knew the old tales of the first people of Q'ara, crossing the Great Southern Desert to the paradise of the northeast, where they had settled in the first Great Trees.

Tala, the All-Mother, had been driven mad with rage at the mirages of waterholes in the midst of crippling, distant heat waves. She led her people from one to the next, watching in horror as every time they got close, the mirage became just another part of the endless sand.

People began to die, choking on the dry air itself, or scooping sand into the mouths of suffering children to give them a quick death, and Tala took all their pain, as was her duty, and made it hers. When she found the Great Trees, it was said her heartbeat became one with them all, a network of life in the glowing, Luminous forest. The thrum of that heartbeat kept Aobia alive today.

In the darkest moments of her Fever, the first appearances of the Orb were so disconcerting, so nonsensical, that Nischia could only think of the All-Mother. When she awoke from her Fever break to Queen Feldra, her soul had felt reinvigorated; she'd felt alive like she'd never felt before. And when she discovered she was a Sleeper and held her glowing hair for the first time in her own hands, she thought of the All-Mother again, in her moment of redemption, among the sweet symbiosis of the Great Trees.

The first weeks of her time as a Sleeper was spent adjusting to the Orb's presence: the life that sang to her from deep within it. Whenever she came home to her small dormitory within the walls of the Residency homes, she tried her best to listen for its call, and learn when to give in to it, or to defer temptation. She would need Koln close by, to pull her out of its hold for however long it took her to learn herself. It was so beautiful and mesmerising to look at, and she found herself sometimes lost in it, gazing deep into its centre, which seemed to carry within it an infinitude she could not put into words.

She saw little of Queen Feldra after assuming her place as a student of the Sleepers, and spent much of her time instead with Koln, the disgruntled tutor she had been assigned to. Koln hadn't shared much of himself with her—all she knew was that he was a superior in the Magisterium, and that he was older than many others there, though the Blessing of the Tree did not make him appear as such.

Koln's lessons were quick, and often unassuming. He taught her about the Blessing of the Tree itself, and how it "chose" Aobians, based on the greatness in their very genes. She preferred a more logical explanation, though with him, she found none. He was a zealous believer in the gifts the Tree provided to Aobia and would not entertain the thought that there was any science behind the Sleepers' abilities to generate and use Luminosity.

Less than a week into her lessons, Nischia met the first and only other new student, a Sleeper named Prisma. It had seemed through coincidence alone that they had both turned through the Fever on the same night and came into the fold of the Magisterium on the same day. When Nischia spoke to Prisma for the first time, she knew she would no longer be alone.

"Sisters," she breathed. "We're sisters of a kind, aren't we?"

Prisma's eyes smiled. She had enormous blue eyes, and carried with her a sunny disposition, enough to make Nischia forget it was wintertime.

"Sisters." She nodded. "How thankful I am to have someone close. I was so scared. The Fever, it ... took everything from me. I thought that I was surely dead."

Nischia peered at her, taking in her story. "Your family, did they...?"

"They know," Prisma said stiffly. "Though I cannot see them. Loche will not allow it. He said the life I live must be separate from them for a time, until they and I can recover from the loss. I need to understand that this vocation has been assigned to me by the Tree, and that cannot allow for family." She tried to grin, an audible swallow sounding as she finished.

"A vocation," Nischia said, stifling a crude laugh. "That's what they call it, even though we all supposedly bear the free will to choose the life we want. The more I think about it, the more I feel trapped. I cannot see my family; I cannot leave the Tree if I wish ..." She shook her head dismally.

"If you wish?" Prisma asked, confused. "You would wish to leave? We cannot live outside the reach of the Tree, sister. Surely you were taught that?"

"Of course." Nischia pursed her lips. "But teaching someone something does not reinforce a belief. They told me my family would not wish to see me again, Prisma. They told you that you could not visit yours. Somewhere along the line, the truth we now live is stitched together with lies. Canopies above, can't you see?"

Prisma recoiled as though she feared being seen near Nischia at all, and Nischia let out a heavy sigh. These thoughts were not allowed. This was not the way to think. But then, when she had just about given up, Prisma reached for her hand, taking it in her own.

"Sister, we have been uprooted from everything that we love. We have been thrown the responsibilities of the highest order of our people, the kinds of people Aobia tells stories about, and covets like demi-gods. We have made a messy and disordered transition from one life to another and lost everything in the process. But ..." She spoke carefully next. "We must strive for hope. For a thread of something, anything to hold onto in this new life. There is joy to be found down every path, Nischia. The teachings I was raised on do not give me belief. But the quest for joy in this life of ours does. One cannot exist without the other."

It was three months into her tutelage under Superior Koln that Nischia had to fight to find a shred of dignity owed to her, when she was granted the chance to visit her family.

"And if I go back to see them, you won't hold it against me?" Nischia asked, bewildered at Koln's mere suggestion. "You won't make me work twice as hard when I return?" She said it with a dash of cheek in her thin smile.

Koln pursed his lips. "You have the full day to do with it what you will. As long as you're back before the next morning, I don't care."

She snorted softly. He could be so disparaging sometimes.

"I'm disparaging because I hesitate to bestow an expectation upon you that might not be met, Nischia."

"Stop doing that," she snapped. Every time he or another Sleeper poked at her mind, she felt open, humiliated. Naked.

"I'll stop as soon as I see a development in your shielding abilities," Koln replied. "You've Slept beyond what you've needed every time I've seen you for testing. Before you question me, question yourself. It is the only way."

"So I don't disappoint myself," Nischia said automatically, under her breath.

"Exactly," Koln responded, curt. Finally, when she said nothing more, he sighed. "You must understand, child. They will not take you back. Even if they do, even *if* they are slightly cordial towards you—they will not receive you as their own. Not anymore. Believe me when I say, I've seen it enough times now to know. The common folk and us ... we all like to pretend we are the same. But the truth is they will not accept you, and you will learn that to make changes in this world means accepting yourself first."

She turned her back on him, blinking back the tears. She had to try, didn't she?

Koln exhaled slowly. "Yes, Nischia. You have to try." He held out a somewhat comforting hand for her to take, and she peered at him as she took it. "Let us be going, then."

They held eyes longer than Nischia felt comfortable, but she wanted to see what he really saw, what he somehow *knew* would happen when she went back home. Feldra and Koln had told her, the day she awoke from the Fever, a newly blessed Sleeper, that her parents had said they did not wish to see her again. She hadn't believed them, but she also knew she didn't want to find out the truth. Not then. Not now, either, if the truth was to be the one she feared most. And she could never forgive herself; not if she knew she would have to live without them.

Eventually, she nodded her head with firmament. "Yes," she said. "Let us go."

They took a cabriolet with two small ponies to tout down the road from the Mind to the Heart, where Nischia's family lived. Nischia balked at the two creatures, tied to the carts. She'd never seen one before; they were bred for the Sleepers' use only and kept in the lower branches of the Mind. The journey took a couple hours, in which time Nischia considered the Aobia she saw beyond the cart doors carefully, as though noticing parts of it for the first time. The *clop, clop, clop* of horse hooves worked in sequence with her heartbeat, and she found herself oddly at ease.

"You are taking the time you need to settle yourself," Koln said. "I can tell. It's not easy to do, but Sleep can help with that, too. Sometimes our greatest challenge is quieting our minds, and the Blessing gives us the fruits we need to do that."

"Not just the Blessing, I'm sure," Nischia said sourly.

Koln sighed. "People out here," he gestured to the world around him, the streets of the Heart that they now drove down, "do not always live the life we want for them. Anxiety riddles us all, though I daresay we deal with more of it than the common folk."

Nischia felt her cheeks grow red with heat. "What a grossly narrow-minded thing to say, superior."

Koln sucked in a quick breath, before retorting, "You will regret the moment when you see I am right, child. There are no emotions in these words, just the facts. The weight on our shoulders is great, as though together, we carry the Canopies themselves. And we do it for *them!*"

Nischia kept quiet then, though she couldn't help but wonder as the shade of the streets changed from vivid colours of dappled sunlight, green leaves, and lively streets, to a dismal, washed out monotony of run-down homes and dirty footpaths, whether Koln harboured a bitterness that he kept deep within, some remnant of pain from years before. *One day, I'll find out what it is that's within him,* she thought loudly, enough to cause his ears to prick up, but not enough that he felt the need to search her mind himself.

The street they turned into was so eerily familiar, and yet equally as foreboding as the horses drew to a stop by the porch of a branchrendered home with one half of the roof collapsing and a haggard door swung ajar in the early winter breeze. The sound of coughing carried out from inside the house to the street, yet Koln's face remained expressionless as he stepped out of the cab, waiting expectantly for Nischia to do the same.

"I'm waiting, child." He tapped his foot on the ground.

Nischia let out a long breath. This was it. She craned her neck to see into the open door, the coughing still being the only semblance of a welcome coming from within. Mother's cough. The one she'd had since she was bedridden the first time, never to get up and about again.

Koln opened the door, beckoning for her to step out beside him. "It's time," he pressed, more gently this time.

Nischia nodded, her body going oddly numb, as though her limbs were moving mechanically, with no help from her own mind. She walked towards the door, while Koln waited behind her. "When you say we leave, we will leave," he said. "Do you understand?"

Nischia stared unwaveringly into the entrance hall, which was littered with things. Rubbish that Father had collected for years, accruing in bulk and taking up all the space for feet to walk within the tiny home. "Yes," she murmured, stepping beyond the doorway, into a life that she could recall being in so recently, and yet now felt like another storyline—a different person's destiny.

The moment her shoes touched the scratched hardwood floorboards, Rili appeared from around the bend, in the direction of their bedroom. Well, only Rili's room now. "Rili?" Nischia whispered, a small squeak escaping her throat. She could practically touch her sister. She *needed* to touch her, even if it were only by the fabric of her clothes. To know she was real.

Rili took an unsettling step back, unsure. "Nischia?" Then she raised her voice. "Mother! Father! Nischia's home. She's home!"

"No, Rili, don't—" Nischia started, racing forward to cup her overexcited sister's mouth. She would cause a stir if what Koln had told her was true.

But it was too late, and the wide, long legs of her father, a stout Aobian in his middle years, appeared next, casting a shadow over the two children. "Nischia," he said, disbelief rendering his face. "As I live and breathe." His voice broke, but his eyes ... his eyes were filled with the darkness that always haunted them. The darkness of the drink. The smell of it reached out to her from his breath, though he stood a couple of metres away. She'd always thought that he was menacing; here, as an outsider, she truly knew what that felt like now.

"Who's this, then?" he asked gruffly, pointing at Koln, and pulling Rili in close to him. He took a protective stance. "You folk said you'd collect her. Now you've brought her back?"

Koln stood in the doorway, blank-faced. He did not frown, his signature expression, nor did he speak. He was not here to speak to them. Nischia understood now. "Th—this is my superior, Father," she stammered. "I wanted to see you, and he brought me here."

"See us?" Her father's eyes searched around the dark home, darting to and fro. He did not want her here, but he didn't want to say why. Koln was right all along.

Nischia bit her lip. "Is Mother well?"

Her father sniffed, an uneasy smile on his face. "I'll take you to her, and then you'll be going. You've got much to do, I'm sure." Rili opened her mouth to speak next, but her father put a finger at his own lips. "Hush, little one."

The door to her parents' room squeaked as her father opened it. "Eanif? You've got a visitor."

Her mother's head sat upright from the sweat-matted pillow, gone yellow with overuse. She looked tired; not in the sense that her health was physically poor, but in the sense that her very existence fatigued her from the moment she woke up each morning. A chronic, sorrowful life. How much of it was created by her, Nischia would never know. The line between her mother's fault, and what injustices had been done to her had blurred over the years, since they lost Mosche.

Her mother's eyes were sharp and severe, and when she spoke, it filled the long, awkward silence with a sound so piercing it dizzied her. "You."

Nischia stepped into the doorway. "Mother," she said, holding back the burn of new tears.

"No! Get away! Away, horrid thing. Away! Regrick, get her out of here, do you hear me? Out!" she wailed senselessly, and Nischia felt her father's arm sweep her out of the room, so that she could only see her crazed mother from a distance, obscured by the partially open door.

"We don't want you!" Mother said, her voice escalating. "You're diseased. You belong with them now. Take your 'Blessing' and leave us. Do you not understand? Leave!"

"But Mother!" Nischia cried, her heart breaking in two. How could they gaze upon her like this? Like she was … smaller than dirt? What had she done? Tears rolled down her cheeks, a flood like the rushing River Tomei below the Great Tree.

Her mother's fevered cries became more frantic, and she panted, running out of breath. "You disgust us. You are nothing compared to Mosche. Nothing! You never will be! Turn away, and leave! LEAVE!"

Her tears were exhausted about halfway through Mother's tirade, and now, Nischia simply hung her head and admitted defeat, the insults washing over her, becoming one and the same. Then the last one came, and she knew she would have to take her leave, of her sister, and her parents. Forever.

"Disgusting." Mother waved her hand flippantly. "Another insidious curse on our lives. A curse!"

Father was still saying nothing, sipping the brown glass bottle he'd been cradling when Nischia had first arrived. Even if he did seem to care, he certainly was not going to let on. Her mother ruled the house, and his heart, and she knew that. She knew that well. A sick, despicable thought grew in her. *You did this to him,* she thought between clenched teeth. *You put the bottle in his hands!* In that moment, it no longer mattered that her crazed, irrational mother wanted her gone. The distance of her father, however, was enough to set her heart to stone.

"Anyone opposed to our life cannot be considered a part of our heart, our home. A waste of time, all along, it appears. A waste of our lives. Take whatever you have left and go!" Her mother waved a flailing hand, and her father obeyed her manic gesture, closing the door. Rili had run off in the chaos; she was nowhere to be seen.

Nischia hesitated, though she did not want to do so in any obvious manner before either of her parents. But this was it. The moment the road truly diverged, away from them, for a lifetime ahead of her that held any number of possibilities. She could be pragmatic, but she could not be an optimist at the same time. Not when her family was no longer considered a part of any of those possibilities. She headed down the hallway, silently, and stepped off the front porch she had helped her father build when she was young.

As she moved from the precipice between an old home for her heart, and a new one, she remembered her superior's words, louder and clearer than the first time Koln had said them: *"Before you question me, question yourself. It is the only way."*

NOW

2055 AS

NISCHIA WALKED BEHIND THE footsteps of Arondil and Garv, the two commanders, watching their ridiculously different-sized footprints form in the snow. The start of the track along the escarpment was a wide ridge, where Sergeant Cavtil had dropped the unit off, and the visibility that the snow seemed to shun meant seeing in front of themselves was a burdensome task. If she lost the footprints before her, Nischia knew she would be in trouble, and so would they; lost, or worse.

Before the two commanders was the smaller group of trackers, made up of both Arv and Riv, the Nestlers, and the twin Aobians, Valton and Gest, who were less alike in their base appearance than was common for twins, but whose mannerisms and expressions were uncanny in their alikeness. They led the unit well, calling out at any point that the path changed direction suddenly, or shrank in size. They'd been moving for a few hours now, but Nischia was sure that if the day was clearer, they would still be able to see where they first got onto the path. If a blizzard came through, which was wont to happen at this time of year, they'd barely make it a couple hundred metres in the same time. Or, if it was bad enough, they'd be planted where they stood. She dropped the thought instantly. Best not to tease a worse possible outcome.

Behind her, a sudden shout of excitement roared through the snow, and she whipped around. "Report!" she called out. She needed something. Any kind of confirmation that the person was all right, or otherwise.

Freya burst through the white air, out of breath. "Wes … slipped on an old root from a climbing tree—the kind that seems to be all over the canyons here."

"Is he all right?" Nischia asked, seizing her shoulder. Freya nodded as Wes himself appeared beside them.

"I'm fine." He shrugged. "Just caught me off guard. Best step with intention, I think. I barely trudged for more than a foot before I caught myself on that blasted root."

Nischia knew the kind of tree that they spoke of. A bendy, pliable tree that grew either straight up from the ground, or out the side of cliff faces, shaped to reach skyward by the high-altitude winds. They were similar to the budding limbs at the end of the branchroads in Aobia, twisted in such a way that they themselves became a buffer against mother nature's blow.

Around her, the rest of the party appeared in a tight bundle, the Nestlers up front, surrounded by the remaining Aobians. "What happened?" Tersa asked, striding forth. She put a hand on Freya's shoulder.

"Nothing of much concern," Nischia replied. "Wes here tripped on a jutting root from these climbers."

"You're okay, then?" Tersa said, a touch of anger in her tone. When Wes nodded, she fired back, "Well, make a better effort of suppressing your lady laugh next time!" She shook her head incredulously and stormed off, the rest of the group disassembling quickly and falling back.

Nischia had already told herself to watch that girl. She was thirsty for merit, and too full of pride. She was also not the one in charge here. Lucky Arondil hadn't seen a bit of her outburst, though perhaps the problem began with him. He wasn't an awfully cavalier leader, from her early impressions of him. Give Tersa half a chance, and she'd have him by the balls. Maybe she already did.

Ahead, Arondil and Garv were waiting, inquisitive. "What happened, Lady Sleeper?" Arondil asked.

"Lady Nischia, we must make headway if we are to find a small cave for the night," Garv barked. "This damn path hasn't changed a touch since we got on it!"

"Do not concern yourselves, Commanders," she replied briskly. "We can move again now, at an even pace. *And* an even footing, if you can manage it. It seems one of Arondil's team got his foot wedged beneath an above-ground root. Walk with purpose, and we'll be fine the rest of the way."

Arondil looked away, possibly offended. She hadn't meant it as a slight against his leadership that Wes had fallen; but then again, maybe he couldn't have read it any other way. Another piece of the puzzle here.

Garv tsked and resumed his pace, Arondil following close behind. They might have been a unit who fought on the same side, but Nischia couldn't help but notice the next problem they faced. These people were not united at all. Out here, in the blistering cold and outnumbered well over ten to one, that would be their undoing. She needed to find ways not only to lead them into an inevitable battle with swift success, but to also join them together. To build a culture. As if noticing the height of the cliffside she walked for the first time, occasionally catching glimpses of the deep ravine that ran beneath them, she realised she had her work cut out for her.

THE NIGHT BROUGHT WITH it a chill that only worsened the group's sense of isolation on the lonely ride. They managed to find a shallow crevasse in one part of the cliff wall they were walking alongside, and some space to spread out bedrolls and build a fire. The Nestlers who were in charge of supplies, Arv, Riv and Scov, put together a comprehensive, albeit basic dinner, of toasted slices of stale bread with cheese melted on top and some jerky pieces of venison. It was hardly the kind of food she would opt for at home in the Great Tree, but it would keep her stomach full and her senses sharp. Nischia found it odd when she thought too deeply about the fact that the Hidden Ones were a hunting people at the top of the food chain, more or less, considering they were on average half the height of the beasts they sought after. She imagined how many it might take to track down and kill a deer but was quickly reminded of the ferocity she'd experienced firsthand, fighting beside them on the peak of the Pass.

After they'd eaten, the wind began to blow with a vigour they had not seen during the day; first with a teasing gust, and then violently enough that they had to snow-over the fire, for fear loose embers might light up their belongings. Teeth chattering, they each turned in, Freya insisting she would take first watch, followed by Tersa. Nischia let the twins off the hook, because they were responsible for tracking throughout the better part of the day and would be for the rest of the journey until the group eventually came head to head with the Theradorans. A part of her heart ached at the thought. They, and the front line Nestlers, would no doubt be the first to die.

Rolling over in her bedroll, Nischia watched Freya, shaking in the wind, despite having furs around her shoulders. She knew there weren't enough *cism* in the cart that Wes had stowed in the back of the crevasse earlier that evening, not for the whole journey. But if she could just concentrate some of the Luminosity from *one* of them, enough to warm the girl's bones just a little …

She got out of her bedroll and strode over to the cart, collecting one of the small orbs. "Freya?"

Freya's eyes did not need to wince to make out Nischia's outline, her Sleeper's glow only increased ever so slightly by the *cism*. "My l—lady," Freya said, teeth chattering.

"You look like you need some warmth, child," Nischia said gently. "Do you trust me? I can use some of what is contained in this to help you." She held out the *cism*.

Freya frowned. "I've never seen anything like it until today, m—my lady. Of course, that's how Sleepers move their powers around."

Nischia smiled as she pressed the tips of her fingers into the orb, sitting beside her on Freya's own bedroll. "That isn't quite right. This does not contain our "powers" as it were, but rather, the result of them. We Sleep in Orbs, a kind of supernatural gift provided to us by the Great Tree, and when we Sleep, we are filled with the potential to channel Luminosity. Most of the time, there is no need for it to be used right away, so we store it in this. It is called a *cism*."

"*Cism* ..." Freya let the word roll off her tongue. "It's strange to know these things only now in my life. I've always found it hard to understand why we are never taught more of the Sleepers and their ways, living under their rule."

"The Magisterium does not seek to rule," Nischia began to reply automatically. Then she bit her own tongue, as she lifted Freya's own hand and placed it on the *cism* as well. Light danced within it, poking through the tops of their fingers, wanting to escape. "Actually, the Magisterium would do well to listen to the people more. We never meant to rule like the monarchy once did. But I'll be the first to say we did not fully succeed in that mission. Now, hold tight."

She closed her eyes, feeling for the Luminosity tucked beneath the surface of the *cism,* asking to burst out into the world. She had to keep it restrained, just like when she Slept in the Orb, constantly suppressing its resonance, trying to keep her head above its waters. But slowly, like a trickle from a rusty faucet, she was able to let forth tiny droplets of light, moving them through Freya's hand. She opened her eyes then, fully in control, watching as Freya's shoulders relaxed, and she took a long, uninterrupted breath. The cold had left her. This would hopefully be enough to get her through to the next post, when Tersa would take over the watch.

"Thank you, Lady Nischia," Freya said, her voice dreamy and relaxed. "I've never felt ... anything quite like that. But I can breathe again, and speak without stuttering. It's as if my bones themselves feel warmed."

"It doesn't take much, child." Nischia grinned. "But it's a careful thing. Luminosity is not something to tamper with."

"What would happen?" Freya asked curiously. "If you were to allow more to flow through me?"

"With intention?" Nischia asked rhetorically. "Nothing. Without focusing on it? Well, you could die."

"Die?" Freya said, alarmed. "I thought the light of the Sleepers was just that. Light."

"It is never something we would think to use offensively. But it does not mean we cannot. Take the war, for instance. That battle on the peak of the mountain is gruelling. Every day it decimates our numbers, whittles away at our reinforcements. It's neck to neck. And there aren't enough of us—Sleepers, that is—to use Luminosity as a tool for attacking. When I'm on the battlefield, I hold a sword and shield, like many of us, or in your case, a bow. The *cism* I have access to are for things like light in the dark, or what I've just done to you, and for those who are wounded and in shock. If I channelled the Luminosity aggressively, I myself would grow tired. Maybe worse."

"You'd die, too?"

Nischia felt her eyes darken around the edges as she put the *cism* back beneath her cloak. "I've only once had to resort to using Luminosity in such ways. But die? No. Sleepers receive a much worse fate," she said, grimly. "We burn out, like a dead star in the sky. They call people who do that Remnant Cores. Each Sleeper has a Core in them, some kind of Blessing from the Great Tree, that allows us access to our Orb, that causes our hair—" she fiddled with her locks to punctuate her words, "—to glow like this. When we overexert ourselves, we no longer get to experience the death that is commonplace for others. Instead, we become a hollow shell of what we once were, able to draw on the difference between light and dark, like the very shadow your body casts in the direct beams of the sun. We lose the ability to regulate our emotions. We *want* to die, but we cannot. When this happens to a Sleeper, it is the Magisterium's primary responsibility to ensure that the Remnant Core is removed from society immediately. We cannot allow them access to our people, the Tree, or any of the lands beyond Aobia."

The wind's words filled the silence before Freya spoke again. "Have you ever seen a Remnant Core, my lady?"

Nischia sighed. She shouldn't have given Freya as much information as she wanted. But oftentimes, it was better for her too, to talk about her life, and the strange aspects of Sleeper culture that were lost on other Aobians. Loneliness was a void she'd been all too eager to fill, ever since that first day she awoke from the Fever as a child and accepted her new fate. She decided in that moment to tell Freya the truth, and then bid her goodnight straight after. "I have seen it, once." She bowed her head, overcome with emotion.

Freya narrowed her eyes, apologetic. "It was someone you cared for, wasn't it?" she asked. "I'm sorry, my lady! I didn't mean to ask, I was just—"

"No," Nischia said firmly. "I decided to tell you enough to make you curious. It's not your fault, child. But yes, I cared for them very much. I was one of the Sleepers who ..." She swallowed. "... Who had to capture and contain the queen, the day the monarchy collapsed."

Freya covered her hand with her mouth. "Oh!" Her voice was little above a whisper.

"Nearly a hundred years, Freya. You would not have yet been born."

Freya nodded.

"Ninety-seven years this year since several millennia in history and royal lineage in Aobia collapsed. Despite her crimes, I ... miss her. She saved me, as a child. Helped me to know a new life, and forget the old, as hard as it was. But I will never say I regret what we had to do. And now, the Magisterium is a better government for our people than it ever was." She stood up abruptly, nodding stiffly to Freya. "Well, child, the night goes on. I must get some rest, I fear. I hope I was able to invigorate you enough until your shift is over."

"Goodnight, my la—"

But Nischia had already strode off, the weight of her past heavy on her shoulders. As she settled the *cism* back in the cart, she caught another face in the dark, closing their eyes nearly faster than she could've comprehended.

Tersa. The headstrong child must have heard every little thing Nischia had exchanged with Freya.

Nischia pretended not to notice and got back into the thin cover of her bedroll.

THEN

1958 AS

SHE HAD SPENT THE day in and out of Sleep, being stirred out of it by Koln to stop her from overstepping the boundary into the Orb's depths. He'd told her time and time again that this would be the case for many months, and perhaps a year or longer, until she had adjusted to the grasp of the Orb and was able to resist its call. Using the Orb, therefore, was a complex dichotomy of pushes and pulls, half fighting herself, and half fighting the Orb itself. While it was the catalyst for her access to Luminosity, it was also a sure way to burn out and risk becoming like those Koln called Remnant Cores—Sleepers who had taken too much from the Orb, either out of greed, a lack of temperance, or desperation to draw more Luminosity than they could hold. Aobia's history was dotted with hundreds of these figures appearing over the years, usually as a result of some civil conflict in the country or the sad ending to a corrupt ruler.

"You must both harden and soften your heart, child," Koln told her after pulling her from the hold of the Orb one afternoon. It was her first summer after becoming a Sleeper, and she had still so much to learn about what she could do with the Blessing that had been bestowed upon her. She did not tell him about her failed attempts to dismiss the call of the Orb in the depths of the night when she was at her most fragile and lonely.

But Koln knew that deep within her, armour was growing, like a carapace over her body. A way to deflect the pain of being cast out by her family, or the perfection she constantly strove for but always missed, sometimes by the breadth of a hair, other times a vast lack of abilities getting in the way.

"My heart is not hard," she replied back curtly, trying to measure out her breaths. Readjusting to the physical world was always like that when she came back from the Orb; like the air was thicker than water.

"Your heart is not soft, either." Koln placed a firm hand on her shoulder. "Look at me. I am no harbinger of joy. But I know that joy is the secret, before happiness, before satisfaction. Joy can accompany you in the greatest moments of tribulation. Happiness is an unattainable thing, like a heaven you trick yourself into seizing in your very palm."

Nischia considered this, a deep frown coming over her face. Joy. She felt no joy. What joy could be found when she knew not where she belonged? Where she was needed in this world? Where was joy when she only ever felt detached from everybody else's story?

Koln studied her face for a while, perhaps allowing her the chance to come to some acknowledgement of his words. After a long pause, he spoke. "The Great Tree is not simply a tree, Nischia. It is a conduit to something bigger than all of us. All of this world. The Blessing you have been given is not a small duty to be shirked when it suits you. The gods above have allowed you it, for a reason. In my centuries on this land, I have often questioned what that reason is, for myself. But knowing they are with me, and I am beheld in the outstretched arms of the Tree is enough. Sometimes it's *all* I have. If that cannot bring me joy in the face of each trial that threatens to uproot me, what can?" He sighed, standing from the small chair he had sat on, the one Nischia kept tucked in under her writing desk. "I will leave you now. We have an important day ahead of us, Nischia. Rest, unwind ... maybe consider spending some time with the other students, if they too are free from their mentors. Sometimes I forget ..." He trailed off, a hesitant strain tugging at his words. "I forget you are just a child. And I forget that not everything revolves around our work. I hope you can see that I value responsibilities. I only want you to be successful in responding to their call yourself." Nischia stared at him as he nodded stiffly and left.

THE MAGISTERIUM OF AOBIA met in a grand governmental headquarters in The Mind, which was a series of rooms and chambers that all spiralled around a central auditorium. Meetings were called with various Sleepers involved, for various reasons; however, a weekly government sitting was a requirement throughout the year. The main auditorium held, at its centre, a place for the monarch to sit and speak from, as well as a set of sitting booths for scribes and a lectern for speakers. The most staggering thing about the auditorium, however, was the way that the roof was stylised to reflect the circular arrangement of the seats, which sank down towards the centre stage, while the roof poked upward, filled with beautiful, stamped designs that mimicked the shape of the Great Tree's leaves, ambled in and amongst frosted pieces of glass to let the dappled sunlight in.

But, however much Nischia considered the impressiveness of its size and construction, she couldn't help but feel that beneath the surface, the Magisterium was a clinical and soulless place, perhaps the opposite of what Aobians worked to make of their home and culture. So far, she'd been forced to come and attend Magisterial sittings every week alongside Koln, though upon arrival, she was automatically relegated to the back rows of the auditorium, where all the newly Blessed Sleepers would be asked to sit. This time, she singled out the one familiar face that made her feel comfortable and fought her way down the long aisles until she sat beside Prisma, who was waiting eagerly for the sitting to commence.

"Nischia!" Prisma said, smiling brightly. "I haven't seen you in days."

"I've been busy." Nischia sighed. "Koln certainly doesn't let me get away with any less."

"He definitely isn't my cup of tea," Prisma said. "Loche is kind. And patient. He wants me to succeed." She said this with an obvious redness touching her cheeks.

"Prisma," Nischia whispered. "You can't be going dreamy over your mentor!"

Prisma swallowed audibly. "I've tried to separate my emotions from it, but since receiving my Blessing and beginning a new life here … he has been all that I have."

This was a fascinating explanation of Prisma's experience, and one that did not all align with Nischia's. Again, she felt oddly out of place and misunderstood. Koln was a hard person, steely but strong and confident. She knew he wished to steer her down the correct path. But she felt so alone in all this. Echoes of her crazed mother's words flew about in her mind, finding her at the oddest times: *"an insidious curse on our lives!"*

How was it that Prisma could be so happy? So willing to learn, and so able to become enamoured with the simplest of things, like her studies—or, more irrationally—her mentor?

Her attention was brought to the lighting of the lanterns that were kept on hooks about the centre stage. Several Sleepers in clerical roles came out onto the stage and thrust their fingertips against the lanterns, letting small amounts of Luminosity flow into them, a beautiful purple glow spreading about the auditorium. One of the clerics did not use her fingertips in the same way; instead, she held a small sphere in her hand, transferring the Luminosity within it to the lantern with her fingers on her other hand as a conduit. Nischia had seen one of those before, though Koln had not let her close to them yet. *Cism,* they were called. Small balls of glass that could be used to store a Sleep's worth of Luminosity for use at a later time. This was how Aobia seemed to run, despite the common folk being unbeknownst to it. *Cism* were also the key to the cleansing of the River Tomei's water, which was turned to poison centuries ago.

What had happened, nobody seemed to know. There were significant holes made in the histories of the people that Nischia knew others had tried to fill over the years. But all that they could find was that a great calamity had taken place, much farther south, where the Aobian people had come from. Somewhere along the way, the River had been turned to poison. Considering it was the main body of water on this side of the Theradoran Ranges, it needed to be cleaned. The Sleepers had found ways to do this through Luminosity, and some very advanced processes of filtration that occurred down in the River itself.

There were secrets the Aobian people had held, and now had lost, and they always put a sense of unease in Nischia's mind when she thought too deeply about them.

Across the centre stage, several scribes took their places in the booths, while a speaker rose to the lectern. It was one of the senior advisors to the throne, the People's Minister. Her name was Staril, and she struck fear into Nischia with her ice-cold stare every time their eyes had connected. She was a good friend of Koln's and seemed to know him on levels Nischia was sure she herself never would.

"Esteemed members of the Magisterium, and protectors of the nation Aobia," she began, reading down the length of her nose from a script. Her voice was quiet, and Nischia found herself leaning so far forward to hear her speak that she nearly bumped into the row in front of her. Staril waved to one of the clerical workers and had them bring up a *cism*, perhaps the same one that had been used to light the lantern before. Staril put her fingertips to it and spoke again. This time, her words were so clear and loud they seemed to fill the room and resound within Nischia's own ears like invading thoughts.

"I come to you today to make an announcement I am both heavy-hearted to disclose, and yet obligated by my knowledge of duty and the honour I am bound to in my vocation as a Sleeper for this nation. What I am here to say will, at the least, shock you. At worst, it will drive thoughts, doubts, and cloudy patches of judgement into your soul. You will find reason to question so many parts of your existence here, in this Great Tree, before the sitting is through."

This came as a surprise, and Nischia felt the same weight as the rest of the room, as though a heavy blanket was being shoved over them all from above. Her throat went dry with the rising sense of dread. Koln had not told her about this sitting. She tried to make him out in the crowd, but the back of his head was cast in shadow. Did he know what was to come?

"A crime of irreparable treason has been committed against the throne of Aobia. The queen, Feldra, is not at today's sitting, as you may have noticed. For the foreseeable future, it seems she will not be. It is with every sadness and disappointment that I am announcing that as of today, the throne bears an empty seat, and Feldra, the last in a long line of monarchs, has been placed into the Magisterium's custody for an indefinite period, to be assessed before an Exile Committee in the Supreme Court in the coming weeks."

"What?" Nischia blurted, as the room erupted around her, a sounding board of contention, disbelief, and lamentations. The Queen of Aobia, an exile? An outcast, forced to live outside the reach of the Great Tree, for at least a quarter of the time she otherwise would? People were crying, screaming, and calling for Staril to step down, for the queen to be brought back before them, for—

"SILENCE," Staril's voice boomed, and Nischia pressed her hands to her temples, a piercing sound frequency cutting through her ears as the minister's lone word reverberated around the chamber.

With the room quiet, Staril gave a long and heavy sigh before continuing. Even the scribes were affronted by this news, as word of exile was exceedingly rare, and as Staril went on, most did not write a single word.

"Present here today are two of our finest foreign ministers, and their chosen ambassadors to the Sea Kingdom, with whom we continue our alliance and trade agreements." Staril immediately stepped to the side, as another four figures appeared.

The two Sleepers Staril had confirmed were foreign ministers did not take the podium; this was left instead to the ambassadors, who were still dressed in the clothes of travellers, and had not a glowing hair on their head. Common folk, who were given high-level clearance to travel between Aobia and her allies' territories, to conduct foreign business and maintain diplomatic relations.

"To the Magisterium, esteemed ministers and advisors to the Throne, and the people of Aobia," the first ambassador said, his voice lacking the amplification Staril was able to use via Luminosity. The room now, though, was so quiet, Nischia could've heard a pin drop. "These past few weeks of work in both Adira and Therador have been trying, to say the least. My name is Agnar, and my colleague is Zayna."

He gestured to the short-haired female beside him. "Our latest work took us to both nation capitals, but it was in Adira where we discovered, via an internal leak of information, that the Queen Feldra of Aobia has been exchanging volatile *cism* units for treasury gold. The deals have been kept operating by a corrupt treasurer that has since been removed from office in Adira. The same deals have been made with those who manage the coffers which belong to the Emperor of Therador, and as of today, I cannot provide you with any updates that suggest the deals have been cut off. This poses an enormous threat to our people, as the closely guarded Blessing of Luminosity is being shared in an extremely dangerous manner with humans that do not understand how it works or what it is capable of. Queen Feldra has provided us with evidence since this discovery was made, that suggests she has found a way to keep *cism* intact, but ultimately able to be exposed to humans. The Luminosity transfers to them, but its quality is significantly diminished, both in potency and how long it lasts."

The audience began to talk, one on top of another, before Staril interceded, calling for silence again. "My people," she said, stepping in front of the ambassador, Agnar. "While this is a grievous crime, the risk of Luminosity being granted to humans is low. The tampered *cism* do not provide a long period of time to use the blessing, and what can be used is so minimal, it may not even light a lantern." A sound of partial relief washed over the crowd. "The nature of the crime, however, is deeply deceptive and egotistic. It speaks to a greater attribute of a person who we have come to know and love for centuries, and the low bar they would stoop to for materialistic riches. What further plans Feldra had with the money she was gaining from either nation, we may never know, despite our attempts to find out."

The loudness across the chamber continued, but Nischia couldn't hear a word of it. She drifted to another place instead, where she had learned to harbour the pain of her life and tried to place everything she'd just heard in that same spot. Her memories were kept away, as though they were clothing items, or tidbits, for storing in drawers. Some with locks, some without; she knew when to open them, and when to keep them closed.

Queen Feldra had been the first person to celebrate her receiving into the Sleepers. The first to tell her she could do anything. In many ways, the queen had been an example of the few people in Nischia's life who held any semblance of belief in her. But this? This was unimaginable. The sting of it was so sudden that Nischia felt as though the world had shifted out of place, and she was trying to stand between where it had once stood and where it stood now. Sick to the pits of her stomach, she stood up suddenly, keeping her head bowed low.

"Sister?" Prisma said, reaching for her arm, but Nischia seized it away.

"Let me leave, Prisma," Nischia said, tears rising. "Please let me leave."

She exited the seating row, headed to the end of the aisle that led out of the central chamber, and ran, as fast as a child who was playing a game, toying with their parents. But she wasn't playing a game; instead, she was the one who'd been toyed with.

Again.

NOW

2055 AS

THE MORNING SUN WAS stifled behind the haze of cold, but it pried Nischia awake, nonetheless. She pinched the bridge of her nose, blinking morning grit from her eyes. The Nestlers had already prepared breakfast, a thin tea made with some kind of arid little bush found along the skirting sidewalls of the cliffs. "Energy, Lady Sleeper," said the Nestler called Scov. "The branches of the windbrush are filled with a green, stringy stem that can keep your body alert for hours after consuming it." The small Nestler held out a bowl of the tea to Nischia in tiny paws, which she took with much trepidation. Being an Aobian, she was no stranger to tea; in fact, it was her preference of drink for most times in the day. But this tisane was foreign, as much in smell as in sight, a languid green slick on its surface. The density of it was even odder, as she took her first sip, perceiving something closer in mouthfeel to soup than tea. But the drink did its job, and she was surprised to feel so awake and ready to move soon afterwards.

While she rolled up her things, Arondil and Garv came over to her. "My lady." Arondil nodded. Standing before the striking sun, the light behind him carved a line around his chiselled frame.

"Commanders, good morning," she said, flinging her pack across her shoulders. "Commander Garv, is there a set plan for today? How far have we come?"

Garv frowned. "We haven't gone far, Lady Nischia. The enemy will be moving as fast as they can on the ridge below us. If they meet us closer to this point of the mountainside, Garv fears they will push through to the boundaries of the camp with full momentum."

"I've had a thought," Arondil said. Nischia pursed her lips, listening to him continue. "What if we could find a point along the cliffs, thin enough to dislodge? We could try to block the way."

Nischia rubbed her cheek. "That *was* the original plan, but ... there are so many variables. If we want a strategy, we need to prepare to fight them, surprise them somehow, while still maintaining a position safe enough for us to be concealed."

"The escarpment may eventually wear out and become one with the same ridge they are traversing now," Arondil said. "Who's to say we'll have a place to reinforce ourselves at all? We don't really know what lies ahead."

Nischia began to walk out from the crevasse and back onto the path. "Let me think on it, Commander," she said. "I must not compromise on our safety unless there is no other option. I cannot be responsible for the deaths of fourteen people out of simple negligence. If we find the opportune place and time to try and stage a landslide, we can do so. But the idea alone sounds ludicrous, if I am honest."

Arondil looked taken aback as he nodded stiffly, speechless.

The group progressed along the mountainside well that morning, as the wind and snow had died down to next to nothing, and what warmth they could get from the sun through the trees and the shielding cliff on the other side kept them from growing weary as fast as the day before. Just before noon, however, Valton and Gest had stepped back in line, pausing the group in their tracks. "The path," Valton started, out of breath. "It ends, up ahead."

Nischia and the two commanders headed on with the trackers, making sure to space out the rest of the group behind them, as the path sloped down on a heavy decline, becoming slippery enough that just one misstep would see somebody from the back compacting the whole group into an unstoppable force. She put Tersa in charge of the second group, instructing her to count to sixty before moving them forward.

Valton and Gest were right, however, as the bottom of the path came to an abrupt end, like the mountainside had cut right through it, a deep gorge leading to dense brush and trees below. Another three metres past the sudden slope was a tiny continuation of the path, but it would not be easy to reach, if they could do it at all.

"Well," Nischia said wryly. "That puts a steady stop in our plans."

The irony was not lost on Arondil, who simply shook his head. "Damn. Where can we go now?"

"Lady Nischia," Garv said. "In the supply carts, there are ropes and pickaxes. Garv had not hoped it would come to using them, but Garv fears we have no other choice."

"Pickaxes?" Nischia asked incredulously. "You want us to climb across the mountain's slope? The drop is treacherous, Commander. If someone loses their footing, they'll be lost forever."

Garv narrowed his eyes as if trying to see the other side of the path clearer. "Let us go first, Lady Nischia. Nestlers weigh nothing. If we get across, we know how much the slope can hold. If we fall … may our impact be softer than an Aobian when we land."

Hesitant, Nischia agreed, and Garv headed back to retrieve the rest of his Nestlers. There were only three pickaxes in the store; a tool each might've been desirable but was in no way practical to carry. Arv, Riv, and Scov all took up an axe each, and with the rope braced by the other three, they set off to cross the sloping face of the steep gorge. They scuttled by with relative ease, though their feet had no place for additional purchase. A blast of momentum allowed Arv, up first, to swing his way across, moving the axe each time, leaving the one behind him implanted in the wall for the Riv. Scov held the slack on the ropes that bound his two companions together, until Riv made it to the second pickaxe, at which point Bvil and Garv both took up the extra pulling force to allow Scov across. Before long, they'd made it, and Garv carried a positive expression for what seemed like the first time in his life.

"The rest of us will go now, Lady Nischia," Garv said, handing his rope to Tersa and Hadi who were standing right behind him. The two

Aobians were able to bear the weight of the next three Nestlers without so much as a grunt. Once on the other side, Garv called out to them, "Move the pickaxes, as the first one crosses—they will have taken all they can bear in their current place!"

"I will go first," Tersa said, holding her part of the rope out for someone else to take, and tossing her fur coat onto the snow. There was an edge to her voice, as though she was trying to protect her sense of fear from being perceived by anyone else. *The girl will learn the hard way,* Nischia thought, mentally steeling herself for whatever might come next. Arondil instead took up Tersa's rope and stood back, giving her space to grab the rope that was not woven through the loops at the top of each pickaxe's handle.

The very moment that Tersa's weight gripped the end of the first axe, one foot still holding limply on to the edge of the path, the axe made a grinding sound and slipped, cutting downward through the rock wall and sending small fragments of stone down the gorge. Nischia leapt forward instinctively, ready to grab Tersa's leg at the next sign of slipping.

"It … seems to be holding on!" Tersa puffed, her face contorting as she took her body's weight with both arms, holding the axe. After a minute of tense silence, the combined breathing of everyone adding to the weight of Teresa's climbing, she managed to get across, moving the pickaxes into new spots for the next person to take. The first one, however, still sat crudely in the place where it had fallen through the stone, making it a hard point to spring from to the second axe.

Nischia took up her coat and balled it up as firmly as possible, throwing it over to the other side for Tersa to take back. "Canopies!" she swore. "The supplies, Arondil. What will we do with the supplies?"

Arondil furrowed his brows, not quite comprehending, until his eyes widened. "A stupid mistake. We cannot possibly get the carts across!"

"Wait!" Tersa called from the other side. "There are a number of cloven trees, and some only half so below me. The Nestlers and I can try to retrieve some and build a crossing. We can support it with our combined weight!"

"No," came the voice of Valton, the tracker. "It's suicide." He turned to Nischia. "If they lose their grip, or fall, they're gone forever, my lady."

Nischia grimaced. "It's either that, or we turn back enough that we can find a lower path. But if we do that, we risk being more visible to the Theradorans when they come past us." She stiffened, knowing exactly what they had to do. "No, Valton, she'll just need to try it." The group all stared at her, aghast.

"She could die!" Arondil seethed.

"We could all die!" Nischia yelled back. "To cold, or some other dark force out here. Or to our enemy, when we are placed right in their line of sight! Look down that gorge—do you not think they will come directly past here if they get far enough down the ridge? We need to do what we can to stop them before it's too late. I don't care if we all die, Commander. This is our duty now. We hold this weight. Nobody else."

Arondil blinked at her, and the others remained quiet. Hadi gripped his shoulder with one free hand. "It's okay, Commander. I believe she can do this."

A long, significant glance passed between Arondil and Tersa then, from one side of the path to the other, and Nischia couldn't help but feel frustrated. There was something more to this commander and his soldier.

"It will be all right," Tersa said from the other side, calm as the breeze through the Great Canopies back home.

They didn't belong here. Nischia knew that and felt it acutely. Her people were made for the Tree, and nothing more. And they were all going slowly mad, fighting out on this mountain, away from its reach. The Tree had three parts to it: Heart, Mind, and Soul, and yet Nischia felt her own of those things diminish day by day, so far from home.

Arondil and Hadi kept a firm grip on the rope as Tersa came back across the gorge, the Nestlers counterweighting her by pulling on the rope from the other side. Carefully, she unlooped one part of the rope from the pickaxe handle closest to her, and with a jutting twang, it went down, Hadi and Arondil groaning to keep up the slack. "We need another!" Arondil wheezed. Each of the twins ran up to him and took more of the rope, pulling back again.

"Not too much!" Tersa cried, dangling below them now, in the centre of the gorge. "I need to be lower, so you must unwind the rope—slowly!"

Nischia bit her fingernail subconsciously, closing her eyes to the sound of the rope unravelling, and Tersa dropping even more. Tersa might have been bull-headed, but nobody else had put their hand up for this outrageous plan. She peeked over the edge of the broken path to see Tersa dangling, one-handed, within reach of a set of branches that sat on a small outcrop of rock.

"I need more slack!" she called out.

"Too much more, and we won't be able to get you back up!" called Garv from the other side.

"All right," Tersa panted. "Let me try something." Carefully, she grabbed the rope with her other hand.

"Tersa! What are you doing?" Hadi asked in disbelief. It was the most Nischia had heard from him since they'd met.

Below them, Tersa was using her second hand to support her weight while she wrapped the rope over itself, creating a kind of tourniquet for her wrist. She tightened it enough that she could still hold the rope in the same hand, and Nischia nodded, impressed. The girl had brains, despite how hard her head was.

Able to hang freely, Tersa began to swing, gently at first, and then enough to nearly run the rock wall with her feet. The line-holders, however, were being worn down, and the Nestlers in particular were running out of strength to hold her weight, given that they were a third of the size of everyone else. A Nestler did not even come up to the waistline of most humans.

"Ah! Damn it!" Tersa cried, just missing a sizeable dead branch. Many of the trees here died and went hollow, Nischia noticed, as that was where creatures like rabbits hid to escape their prey. All the wood was light, but extremely hard—a result of having grown in such desolate and cold conditions.

"We're losing our grip!" yelled one of the Nestlers. Nischia watched in horror as they skidded towards the edge, Tersa's pendulum-like swinging pulling them down inches at a time.

"Do something!" Arondil yelled, fiercely leaning back, trying to keep the slack.

It was one thing to handle the weight of a person who was very much able to distribute it across their limbs, applying different muscles at different times. But very quickly, the three on the rope learned what it was like to hold back dead weight, the kind that didn't move. The kind that couldn't move.

While Nischia ran back to the supply cart, thinking of what she could try and do with the *cism,* the rest of the group continued to groan in exertion. She was the ultimate leader here, and it would be on her conscience if anything happened to any of them. While she was a revered Sleeper to the party, she was nothing to herself but a disappointment and struggled to think of how to use Luminosity to keep the rope pulled taut.

All of a sudden, as she was running back to the group, who now saw all the Aobians on the rope, taking up whatever they could to save the Nestlers from falling, a piercing *snap* sliced through the air. Hadi screamed immediately, dropping the rope in shock. "Tersa! No!"

The Nestlers slid, one by one, until only the one named Scov remained, holding on with everything he had. At that moment, Arondil collapsed on the ground, wailing like a child. Hadi paced around aimlessly.

His eyes became like a void, filled with fear, and Nischia dropped the *cism* she held in the snow. "What happened?" she said, gripping his shoulders. Hadi shoved past her, storming off into the snow.

"No," whispered Arondil, who was struggling to look down any longer.

"Help!" cried Garv, the other Nestlers dangling down behind him trying to hold on. "She's dead, damn it, and if you don't pull us back, we will be too!"

Dead. Nischia gasped, kneeling down in the snow. An arrowhead, rusted and crude, jutted out from Tersa's neck, blood pouring from the wound like an open faucet. "They're here," she said to herself first. "They're here! We must move."

Arondil was still leaning over the edge, crying, and Hadi was gone, off into the white haze behind them, but the rest jumped to attention immediately.

"Pull them up!" Valton said, his sister hauling his waist back, while Wes and Freya collected the rest of the rope. Soon, all the bodies came up, including the Nestlers, who were haggard yet happy to be alive.

All except one. Arv, the smallest of them all, lay on the end of the rope, his paw firmly planted in Riv's, who managed to hold him the whole time that they were being rescued. "Riv thought he would—" the Nestler began to croak, his voice breaking. "He didn't make it." Another arrow was stuck in Arv's side, penetrating whatever collection of vital organs lay within. With this wound came less blood than Tersa's, but it was fatal, nonetheless.

"Not another!" Nischia cried, racing over to examine the small-framed creature. She cupped his tiny, fur covered head in her hands, and pressed her thumbs into his neck, hoping for a sign. *Just one sign.* It turned out there was, as the Nestler's eyes fluttered slowly open, and he sucked in a painful breath. "Lady ... Nischia?"

Nischia cradled the Nestler in her arms, knees buried in the snow. "You're okay, Hidden One. Stay with me. The *cism*—I can use the light to heal you." She turned to look at the rest of the group, who were fumbling about in panic. "Coats, blankets, anything! Anything warm."

Arondil had finally stood up. "With respect, Sleeper. You nurture the Nestler back to life, without even checking that one of our own lives. In moments, we may be surrounded by the enemy, and then what?"

A sharp whistle sounded as another arrow struck flesh. "Aargh!" Arondil screamed, falling over. He'd been struck in the shoulder, some-where *from above.* The information they had was wrong. The enemy was not approaching from beneath them.

All this time, they'd had the higher ground.

THEN

1958 AS

THE SOUND OF HORNS was not a natural noise to hear throughout the canopies of the Great Tree, and it only added to Nischia's uneasiness. Stepping off the side of the road, she stooped into some hedges, retching as quietly as she could. What did the horns signal? When she rejoined the road and glanced back at the Magisterium, shivers crept down her neck. Everyone was exiting with a pace nearly equal to hers, running in sporadic directions. She looked around frantically as one part of the crowd rushed by her, hoping to see Koln, but a hand reached for her shoulder first, intercepting her.

"Are you okay, sister?" Prisma said, pulling her into a tight embrace.

Nischia sniffed loudly, her face pressed into the warm cloth of Prisma's light green shawl. "What's going on? What do the horns mean?"

"We must go home, Nischia, now!" she said, nearly feverish in her persuasion. Then suddenly, her face grew very grim, a look Nischia had never seen her only friend sport, like there was a darkness in the world that threatened to consume them all. "The queen," Prisma said in a hushed tone. "She fled the prison, somehow. We are being placed on a high alert."

"No," Nischia started, stepping away from her. "It isn't right, Prisma. She—she's a good person! Not some villain to dethrone and cast out!"

"Nishia, no," Prisma said, shaking her head furiously. "She is no longer our queen. We *have* no queen. Feldra is a criminal, on the run. She's *dangerous,* Nischia. If she was planning on selling our source of power to the humans for so long, she is certainly capable of far greater sins. Can you not see that?"

Nischia stood, stagnant, hearing only the rush of the people down the street. As she began to speak, the horns cut off, their pitch growing dissonant and fading. Then a rumble that seemed to shake the Great Tree by its very roots moved the branchground they were standing on.

An explosion so bright, like that of the sun, or a dying star on its final campaign, spread forth from the Magisterium, shattering its frame and levelling the front of it. The force of it took Nischia's breath away. Prisma screamed, falling below the hedges that lined the streets, her only cover. Nischia leapt on top of her, rolling into the bushes to give them whatever little buffer they could get. What seemed to follow the immediate mushroom of light was a dense, dark cloud, consuming everything from the tree itself, down to the very last drop of moisture at the back of Nischia's throat.

Nischia got to her feet warily, helping Prisma up too, and peering over the hedge. Only then did the impact of what had happened begin to dawn on them. Aobian bodies lay strewn in the streets, like discarded toys from a child's play box. Some were entirely broken or shattered, and the crude tang of vomit rose from the bellows of Nischia's stomach once more as she spied a lady's head, torn from the body to which it had once belonged, rolling down the street with a trail of dense, sticky blood after it. Parts of the Magisterium's great architecture lay randomly all around the place. One pillar had crashed down on a number of bodies, but one Sleeper in particular gasped to get out from underneath, their legs nearly mashed into the branchground beneath them.

"We're under attack!" came a voice, and the people started to clamber about, absorbed in total chaos, displaced by the shock that was setting in. Nischia's ears, she realised, were ringing with a high-pitched frequency, and her arm was dripping with blood, possibly injured in the explosion.

Aobian officers seemed to spring to life out of every direction, swarming the streets like bees upon a flowerbed, searching for the spark that had ignited the catastrophe thus far. It was then the first arrow flew, a brazen, whirring sound through the air, finding its target in an unsuspecting guard's back. Nischia was used to rain in Aobia, but not this kind, though the effects were not dissimilar: this rain sent people sprawling to shelter, or home, or some other place. It divided them, causing some to cower, others to freeze, or to join the fight. This was civil war.

Feldra appeared then, surrounded by blazing hot, white light, feeding through her body Luminosity in its highest concentrations. "Aobia, rise before me!" she screamed in a Luminosity-boosted tone, her voice cascading throughout the Mind, and maybe beyond. A select group of Sleepers seemed to fall into step beside one another, a moving fortress accompanying her every stride. Of course. She had not done this herself. She had bred this defection by corrupting a portion of Aobia's highest citizens to gain what she wanted. Power, and riches? She was already the queen. Nischia looked at her, aghast. What more could Feldra have wanted?

"Nischia, we must go!" Prisma tugged at her sleeve. Feldra screamed again, a wave of light flying out from her like a shard of glass, striking a guard who stood before her, quivering. He fell to the ground in two pieces, unmade.

"Okay!" Nischia breathed, finally relenting.

The two girls ran from the city centre, as guards and Sleepers moved in the opposite direction, trying to establish some kind of counter force to stop the queen. The sounds of death and rage followed them all the way to the massive strip of buildings on the fringe of the Mind and Soul, which made up the Sleepers' residential district. As they raced through the front gardens, a bellowing voice called out her name. "Nischia!"

Nischia whipped her head around, wincing in anticipation of meeting some poor fate.

It was Koln, and she had never seen him like this. The older Sleeper had been weeping, his face streaked with dried tears, his hair frazzled and unkempt. He had clearly been marred in the explosion, his robes tattered in places, and long grazes down both his arms and neck. "Child!"

He ran to her at that moment and held her. He held her like Prisma had, although Nischia felt it differently, understanding that Koln had never held another like this before. On another level, the world around her faded away, as if it were just she and him, standing alone in the garden, and she needed nothing else but his embrace. Perhaps, just *maybe*, he could be the father she no longer had, or something like it. It was so bewildering, she did not even cry.

Koln pulled back, kneeling before her, wiping the hair out of her eyes. "I am sorry. I'm so sorry. I had thought our people better than this. Especially her, Nischia. Especially—I—" He choked back the oncoming tears, stifling them by scrunching up his face into a wrinkled up mess. Nischia didn't know what to say.

"Superior Koln," Prisma said, stepping forward, and for a minute there, Nischia had forgotten she was right by them.

Koln seemed to take a second to register her presence, eyeing her wearily. "Child Prisma," he said, suddenly formal. He stood up, brushing grass off his pants absentmindedly. "There is little time. I must ask you both to do an insurmountable thing. We have no other choice."

Nischia nodded immediately, suddenly feeling rejuvenated by her master's presence. "Okay." She gripped Prisma's hand, the only kind of comfort she knew how to give. While the battle in the streets raged on behind them, she knew that whatever was coming, they only had each other.

IN HALF A DAY, Aobia had been split in two. It didn't matter whether one lived in the Heart, Mind, or Soul; division leached from every branch, and by extension, the hands of every person.

Koln tore through the streets, *cism* in hand, while Nischia and Prisma held a reserve each, in case they were needed. Through the streets of the Mind, the trio ducked, darted, and wove their way to the unknown destination Koln had in mind.

The fighting went on all around, though Feldra was nowhere to be seen now. She didn't need to be once she had successfully broken her people into two. The half that knew of her corruption was a noticeably smaller force. Nischia squeezed her eyes shut as they crossed the main street of the Mind; what was normally a shopping precinct had become a bloodbath, and the smell of wounds, faeces, and more overtook that of the early summer leaves that usually coated everything.

"We must keep going, Nischia! Don't stop running. Don't stop!" Prisma pushed her on, physically running into her back to stop her from stooping in the street to retch again. She'd vomited more during this day than any other time in her life.

"Where are we going, Koln?" she cried out to her superior, who ran ahead.

"We are nearly there!" he called back, a non-committal answer.

Finally, they turned a corner, past a few smaller shops and into some of the densest limbs and branchroads Nischia had ever seen. She'd heard tales of what the forest floor below Aobia was like, and this was the closest she'd come to those descriptions, though the leaves they swept out of their way retained the usual size, nearly as tall as her. The twigs that were jutting out quickly became treacherous, and she found it hard to keep her footing as she held the *cism* tightly against her chest, leaping from branch to branch. She looked down and felt herself grow dizzy. *Don't,* she thought. *Don't do it. Don't look anywhere but forward.* The ground had withered away completely now, and she gulped to think of how far they would fall if they slipped or missed a single twig. Eventually, however, Koln slowed his pace, coming to a stop at a nearby knot of wood that was enmeshed in a thinning branch. It was accessible by twigs around it, but only just. He leaned up against the gnarled outside of the knot, breathing deeply. He put his fingertips to the *cism*. Nischia and Prisma watched in wonder as the light bled through him, illuminating his veins, like the branches of the very tree they resided in. He pressed his other hand to the wood, and immediately, it reacted, unlike anything Nischia had seen before.

The wood slowly retracted, like a knot of string untying itself, allowing in the smallest amount of sunlight they could find, this deep into the Tree. From inside the opening ball of wood came a gasp before a hand suddenly appeared over a wall of timber. "It is you," came a wispy voice.

"It is," replied Koln. "And I rue this day that I thought would never come. I do not come here lightly, Logis."

"Come inside, and be quick," the other voice responded. Koln let the *cism* go, rewrapping it in his robes, before gesturing for Nischia and Prisma to come forth.

The once-knotted piece of wood was so open now that Nischia could see into it as she approached, and she found it wondrous to see it was as normal as any other home. A kitchen, a stairwell to a loft, and a living area quaintly kept, were all that were inside. She held Prisma's hand in her own as they crossed the final stretch of twigs, stepping inside. Before them stood a Sleeper. An old Sleeper.

Her hair was still silver, though a shade darker than what Nischia had seen before, perhaps run through with the odd fleck of grey. Her eyes were kind, though tired, and the glow to her seemed different to the other Sleepers; less intense, as though it too was aging into a deep, soft thing.

"Well, child," she said easily. "I did not think you would bring children of your own."

It was only when Koln responded that Nischia realised the old Sleeper was not talking to her. Despite his unfathomable tenure, Koln was a spark before her dying flame. "Feldra will come, Logis. We do not have much time."

"What?" Nischia said under her breath. "What are you talking about?"

Koln shot her a sharp glare, silencing her immediately. "All-Mother. Is she well enough?"

"I have kept her well, in preparation for this day," Logis replied. "If this burns her out, our line will end thereafter."

Koln nodded solemnly. "It is the only way."

"I know, child," Logis replied. "I've always known."

Logis rose up the stairwell to the loft that overlooked the rest of the house. As she did so, Great Leaves and twigs wrapped around them, closing the walls, and returning the secret home to its original state. What was this place?

The trio rose with her to the top, where the emanating glow of an Orb sat in the back of the room. Nischia immediately thought it was Logis's, until she stepped forward and put a hand to the Orb, speaking to it.

"Mother," she said. "You must awaken, Mother. Please. It is time."

Even Koln sucked in a long breath as Logis sat, speaking to the Orb for what seemed like an age. Slowly, though, it began to shudder, the light within it rumbling, vibrating, and forking around the inside, like the brooding beginnings of a storm. The storm rose to a quick crescendo, as the Orb swelled, nearly filling the loft. Nischia stepped back to the rail that met the edge of the loft, pressing herself into it, while Prisma found a small portion of the only untouched corner of the room. The Orb was growing in volume now, a sizzling, frenetic kind of sound, dissonant in all the wrong places, but oddly satisfying in all the right ways. Like when Nischia had been awoken by her mentor, time and time again, and she was pulled out of Sleep, rejuvenated with lively Luminosity.

The sound and the brightness of the Orb was mesmerising, until it vanished, shrinking quickly back to its original size, a quiet, glowing ball in the corner of the room once more. Only this time, a person lay on their side, groaning, struggling to sit up.

Logis threw herself down to the ground. "Mother!" she cried.

The person was not quite Aobian in the traditional sense. Though she was very tall, and glowed like no other Sleeper Nischia had ever seen, she seemed to sag, her back arching over, her shoulders rolled inward. From her skin grew odd stumps, thorns, and leaves. Like she was a part of the Tree itself. Nischia felt fear reach into her mind when she caught the person's eyes, which were a vivid red, coursing with fury.

"You ... awake me from my slumber?" the person asked, their voice razor sharp.

"Mother, please," Logis begged on both her knees, helping the person to their feet. "The day has come. You always knew it. It's like you told me when I was a child. The elect will only fall. Today is the day, the day pride is met with steel!"

"The streets are a war zone," Koln said urgently, stepping forward, but Logis cut him off from moving any closer, blocking him with a strong arm.

"And who ... is this Sleeper?" the person croaked, their voice spliced into three different tones.

"A friend," Logis replied quickly. "He is only here to help, Mother."

"A friend." The person finally rose to their feet, groaning with an exertion that seemed to suggest they were older than an age. "I have not had a friend in this Tree for centuries. Now I have been stirred from my peace. Do you lie, daughter? Do you mean to use me and cast me aside?"

"No! No, Mother. I would never—" Logis began, but she was quickly cut off.

"Hush. If I am to save these people another time, like my mother before me, I must reserve my energy. I will not be tested again. Now, who is this Sleeper, and the young ones he has brought to this secret place?"

"All-Mother," Koln began, prostrating himself before her. "I am Koln, a Sleeper of the Magisterium. I was the student of your daughter, Logis. I come in trust, and fellowship."

"Fellowship," the All-Mother said, rolling the word around as though she was tasting it.

Nischia shivered, looking to Prisma. It had clicked for them both, it seemed. This was the All-Mother, the second generation of daughters of Tala's bloodline, the first steward of the Great Trees. This was Raece. She stood there before them, more than a thousand years old, double any other Aobian. She contained all the secrets her own Mother knew, of the connection the Aobians shared with the Tree. Nischia suddenly felt she was in a very sacred place, and became aware of her lousy stance, pressed into the guardrail. She straightened her back, and stood with all the pious expression she could muster. The All-Mother noticed, and settled her old, ruby red eyes on her, with a sad type of longing that Nischia could never understand, though she felt it all the same.

"This child you bring here," the All-Mother said slowly. "She is determined. She is steel." Koln said nothing in return, as the All-Mother drifted like a ghost across the floor, towards Nischia, who couldn't help but shrink back slightly, in fear.

"We are not so different, you and I," the All-Mother said, stroking Nischia's cheek with a long, wobbly finger. Logis stood close by, as though waiting for her mother to fall over, ready to catch. "Do not let your heart go as a stone, steel-child. Nothing can stop you anyway. Why be the only one who can?"

Nischia frowned then, and wondered what the All-Mother saw in her. "I belong nowhere, and to no-one, All-Mother."

"You belong here, in this Tree. It is your vocation. Look at how you glow. Do you not know how many others in this Tree would wish to glow like you? Do you see you have been Blessed, not afflicted?"

Nischia went to speak again, but the building suddenly shook. Like the first time it had opened its concealed secrets to her, Koln and Prisma outside, it began to unfurl, like a cloak about a shadowed person in the night, or an old skin from a cicada. This Tree was alive.

"The time has come," the All-Mother said, stretching her back in an unusual contortion. "If I never rest again in my Orb, I will know at least, somewhere deep within, that I did my duty."

NOW

2055 AS

As THOUGH A SIGN from the gods, the wind began to howl, stirring up a blistering blizzard on the tiny escarpment. Through the kicked-up whirlwinds of settled snow, arrows pelted down onto the crew from above as they struggled to go back, ducking beneath every over-peering rock wall they could as they moved.

"Move!" Arondil yelled through the storm. He carried Tersa's body over his shoulder, like a sack of vegetables, unable to let it go as his shoulder bled profusely onto the snow. The arrow still jutted out through the skin of his shoulder, but his sorrow seemed to numb the pain. Garv led the Nestlers as they held Arv and kept a shawl about his head, so he could breathe in lieu of the storm. Nischia was right behind the trackers, unable to see a thing past their backs.

"Turn back!" cried Gest through the tearing blizzard wind. "The way is lost!" She pulled her scarf back up over her mouth, gripping Valton's hand, who, as usual, said nothing, but Nischia could see the fear in his eyes. The path headed back the other way had begun to collapse, a series of dislodged boulders skidding down the mountainside with a great, rumbling sound. If they wanted to live this day, they would have to fight here, and now. They could no longer retrace to their position from the morning.

"Hold fast!" Nischia roared to the rest of the group over the blitzing wind, which had started to catapult them with tiny shards of ice from every direction at once. She cried out in pain as a sizeable piece whipped her cheek, slicing the tight, dry skin right open. It was so cold that when she removed a hand from the wound, not a drop of blood came.

"Lady Nischia," Arondil said, stepping close to call into her ear. "We cannot fight here. We are dead if we do not move."

"We have no choice, Commander," Nischia said through gritted teeth. "This is the path we've deigned to travel, and it ends on both sides of us."

Arondil begrudgingly stepped away from her and strode over to the cliff face, where he laid Tersa under the loose protection of some shrubs, which hung out from it. He went to the supply cart, wrapping his shoulder in rags, before retrieving a bow and quiver full of arrows and striding off into the vacuous unfolding of infinite white before them. He might have been a metre in front of her, but Nischia didn't know it. He would have to head up the group until there was enough space on the ridge for Valton and Gest to make their way past.

Suddenly, the higher-pitched cries of Nestlers clawed through the coarse hiss of the blizzard, sending a strike of fear through Nischia's chest. She ran forward, pressing each member of the team up against the iced-over wall of the cliff so she had barely inches to dance past them on. She had promised Cavtil she'd bring his team back alive.

Just as she managed to clamber ahead enough to see the capes of the Nestlers flapping in the wind, Arondil seemed to skid, so quickly she couldn't react fast enough to match the speed of him, soaring off the side of the path. "Arondil!" she cried, leaping forward, but an arm held her fastened back.

"No!" screamed a voice, holding onto Nischia's left arm with all her might. It was Freya. "Lady Nischia, if he is gone, he is gone for good. Do not make the same mistake as him. We cannot see where the path ends and the fall begins." She looked at her with pleading eyes. "Come back."

Silence drew its long breath, like a wave over them all. Nischia heard nothing but the thrum of her heartbeat, and her eyes settled only on snow or the white sky. There was no in-between. There was no mark for where Arondil stepped his last living foot.

There was no mark.

An arrow whooshed past her at that moment, separating one part of her swinging hair from another, a finger space from touching her scalp. She felt the air of it through the blizzard, a precaution that what might come next would not be as forgiving. She scuttled back up the path to find Wes holding Freya, and Valton holding him. Gest had already lined up several arrows, firing two at a time off her bow, into the dense white overhead. She had no target, and every arrow seemed like a prayer. *Canopies above, intercede for us!* Nischia thought, desperate.

She clambered through the snow to where the supply cart sat, which was right by Gest's side. The others began to frantically collect their weapons and lob arrows into the sky. Some met the cliff wall with a dull *thunk,* while others seemed to disappear into the void of the storm. If they came back down, would they rain upon their keeper?

Nischia tried to concentrate. Everything was slipping away from her. *She* was the one who promised to bring these soldiers home safely. *She* was the one responsible for stopping the Theradoran flankers. It was always her. Everything fell on her. Her memory flashed as she relived her brother Mosche's death, her separation from her family ... her capture of the queen, the most successfully laid plan, yet the most excruciating moment of her life. All these memories passed her by in seconds, while she reached into the supply cart to retrieve a *cism.* There were only three left. She put her fingers to one in an instant, feeling the rush of warm light go through her. The painful memories returned, running on an endless loop. If she could silence them, and all her iniquities, pressing at her from all sides, she might be able to use the Luminosity to see through the whiteness.

All around her, the storm hailed on, snow occasionally interrupted by volleys of arrows. She heard the characteristic balk of pain as somebody got struck—but she couldn't let herself be distracted by it. She had to go into herself, relinquish her fears. She felt the Luminosity welling up inside her, but she could not direct it—just like the path they found themselves trapped on, the light had no channel to travel here either.

Mosche dying.

Her own mother, casting her out.

The look in the eyes of the only person to have truly loved her, when she brought down their monarchy, and made public their crime.

"Do not think that by hardening your heart you can accomplish your every goal in this life, child."

Feldra's words echoed in her mind as she groaned, trying to push the light through her, so she might use it to see. She had to *see*. From outside, she heard voices, muffled and panicked, calling to her:

"Lady Nischia!"

"My lady, please! The path is collapsing; we must go!"

"I can't move her ... Valton, help me carry her!"

"She's like a stone!"

It was all noise, threatening to take her away from this final place of reckoning. She could not let herself return to the world, not now. Not when there was a chance. She was so close, but the next words nearly stopped her in her tracks. *"Before you question me, question yourself. It is the only way."*

Question yourself. All this time, she had not listened to her mentor. Nischia should never have questioned her validity, or her place in anyone's journey through life. Self-mastery did not come from deprecation. The light rattled around inside her, and she shuddered.

Self-mastery came first with self-forgiveness.

I CAN SEE.

The Luminosity within her worked its way to her eyes, and she could both see the world from within them, and outside them. She looked through the blizzard, around at the screaming, wounded bodies of her teammates. Above her, her enemies did not know the vengeance she could exact upon them. She felt the burn, the adumbrating sense of soothing together with it, as Luminosity welled up in her limbs, forcing her to outstretch her hands. Her hair began to glow fiercely, and she noticed all the crew staring at her in awe or fright. She was a weapon, a crude weapon, ready to take her Blessing from the gods to her enemies.

In a single release of burning white Luminosity, the side of the mountain exploded. A spray of rocks flew out, and down the cascading debris came the bodies of thick-coated men and women, their weapons lost to the air, their limbs crushed, their heads ground to a paste in seconds. Time seemed to freeze as Nischia calculated what would come next.

Suddenly aware of what she'd done, she felt the Luminosity drop from within her like a fire, snuffed out. She crossed her eyes to the closest person to her, Freya, who was clinging on to Wes by the waist. The sea of titan mass crashed into them in a flurry, and everything changed from white to blitzing black.

Sound hammered at her, and she felt the impact of several things at once: feet, heads, rocks, dirt.

The great leveller in this war was perhaps the very place they fought upon.

THEN

1958 AS

THE WAY THE ONCE-QUEEN of Aobia fumed when she entered the hidden home was the first marker Nischia had of who Feldra really was. Until this point, Nischia's heart had felt broken in the wake of yet another betrayal.

"All-Mother!" Feldra roared, light blazing through her, rendering her nearly translucent.

"Ah, the child seeks to disturb me from my charge," was all the All-Mother said.

"The Aobia I built, over centuries, will not come crashing down overnight. I will not allow it. I am the queen elect!"

The All-Mother, despite her wise, aged eyes, smirked a little. "That's right. You were elected to lead my people from hindrance to health, and I supported the vote. I do not support your tyrannical upstaging, Feldra, nor your lack of vision. How short-sighted and immature you must be to share secrets of our Blessings with the outside world."

Feldra's body hummed with power, and she seemed to shake in her place, not with fear, but with an uncontrollable tempest of fury. "Old husk," Feldra whispered, causing Logis to put a hand to her mouth in shock. Nischia had never heard the term before, but she gathered it was nothing less than insulting. "You no longer have the strength to defy me. My Aobia is a safe harbour for my people. We Name people at birth, and we keep them secured in the Tree. Any other life is the antithesis of who we are. Even your own mother knew that!"

All-Mother shook her head. "This was not the world my mother envisioned." Her red eyes grew a bright orange then, the colour of flame, and she tilted her head back, her jaw opening an unnaturally wide distance. The sound she let out was a primal scream, something that echoed through a long and difficult past. Nischia felt it in the deepest places, seeping out the cracks of her heart. Even Feldra, in all her radiating might, shielded her eyes with an arm, stepping back.

"No! Mother!" Logis cried, stumbling over to the All-Mother, but she could not get close. The All-Mother rose in the air, levitating off the ground by inches, outstretching her arms, like dying roots searching for their final quenching drink. Around her, Luminosity spun like silk, preventing Logis from getting close. Feldra screamed back in defiance, balling up hot light in her palms, like she somehow had the power to wield the sun itself.

Koln uncovered his *cism*, calling out to Nischia and Prisma to do the same. "When I give the command," he shouted, "absorb the *cism*. Let it flow through you and fill you up!"

For the briefest moment, Nischia swore the fallen queen of Aobia had caught her eye, and within it, she saw the disturbed soul of a person who had sold it for greed. Feldra was reclaiming what she thought was rightfully hers, and she would take down anybody who came up against her in an instant. But somewhere within her, the kind, caring queen who had helped Nischia feel some belonging after being torn from her family remained. Nischia could see it, like a tremble in the queen's face, a quiver in her mouth, as Luminosity filled her so completely that she became as bright as the All-Mother was, enclosed in her cocoon of light. Nischia still remembered Feldra's words, the first time she had realised that Feldra was the queen. *Why not just be a people, a wave of innovation, of love, and culture?*

It was all a lie, as it turned out, and once more Nischia felt a part of her heart go black with the rot of betrayal. Feldra's hunger outweighed anything before her.

As her thoughts spun wildly around inside her mind, Nischia watched aghast as the All-Mother's strange encompassing of light grew to fill nearly the entire home, light perforating even the most solid of walls like an injection of golden liquid. Koln was placing his fingertips to his *cism* now, watching carefully as Feldra tried to release her raw Luminosity at the All-Mother, who only absorbed it with a howl, using the power to increase her own perimeter.

Koln stepped to the side as energy blazed forward from Feldra's hands once more, enough concentrated light to cause a splash of embers to appear on the walls. "No fire!" he cried. "There will be no fire!"

Fire. Nischia had never seen the stuff, the antithesis of the Tree and its people. Fire was a curse on the land, a thing of death and destruction. Humans argued it gave them warmth, but what warmth did one need, this high up under the Great Canopies?

"This is madness!" Logis cried, reappearing behind her mother with a *cism* of her own, instantly activating it with her fingers. She darted around to where Nischia stood with Prisma and Koln and reached out a hand to Prisma. "Hold my hand, child! Superior Koln, we must do it now, or suffer disaster!"

Koln nodded, an increasing furrow of worry spreading across his forehead. "On your call, my lady. Nischia, take my hand."

Nischia did so immediately, shooting a glare of concern at Prisma, whose eyes were full like two blue moons. Both apprentices held *cism* now, fingertips primed against their surface. They stood facing the incredible power of Feldra and the All-Mother, who were exchanging blows of light.

"Let it flow through you now," Logis said soothingly, trying herself to steady her own breaths as Nischia and Prisma did the same, sensing the foreign Luminosity of the *cism*. It felt like grating pebbles forcing their way into Nischia's veins, compared to the enveloping warmth and honey-like light of her Orb. But the glass *cism* had a purpose.

The *cism* in her hands seemed to tremble as Nischia felt the light slowly making its way into her, as though there was some blockage at the point of transmission, threatening to shatter the glass ball from within.

"You must breathe, Nischia!" Koln shouted over the pulsing burst of Luminosity that Feldra kept launching at her foe.

"I'm … trying!" Nischia gasped. "It's not … I'm not …" *Good enough. I'm not good enough.*

Prisma spoke to her from the corner of her eye. "Sister, you can do it. Just breathe, Nischia. Just *breathe*."

Nischia listened as Prisma's own inhales became longer and deeper, and she stood in a nearly meditative stance, despite doing so in the wake of the corrupted queen's Luminosity attacks.

Just breathe. Nischia tried to slow her heart, but it beat furiously. *One,* she thought, counting as her last resort. Feldra screamed as parts of her body became a disturbing black, her fingers and arms changing to something more akin with obsidian than skin. Light continued to fly forth from her in flurries, whipping across the All-Mother's defensive ring.

"This is futile, fallen child," the All-Mother hissed, her voice oddly sounding like multiple voices at once. "You are burning like a dying star!"

Two. Nischia felt her heartbeat relaxing slightly, as the tingle of awakened Luminosity kicked up inside the *cism.*

"Hold fast, both of you!" Koln uttered, his focus entirely on Feldra.

"She is burning up!" cried Logis. "We cannot face a Remnant, Koln. We do not have the power between us. I fear Mother will not be able to hold on for much longer!"

Three. A Remnant Core. Nischia tried to let her fear wash over her. It didn't matter now. All they could do was try to apprehend Feldra before she tore through the rest of Aobia, and potentially risked starting a fire in the Tree.

Four. "I can't!" She began to cry. "I can't do it!"

"No!" Koln shouted at her. "You must do it, and you *will*. We cannot win this fight without you, child. *Focus*."

Five. She gritted her teeth, trying again to soothe herself. The background noise seemed to relent, fading away, and for a moment, she was able to hear only her steady heart, slowing, slowing. The tingle returned, and the gateway between her fingers and the *cism* opened this time, flooding her like the rush of a river. A river of gold.

"You did it," Koln breathed in disbelief. "You did it, child! Keep the Luminosity alive in you. Stoke the fire and career it around your body. Let it fill you and prepare it for its escape into the world. Now, we fight. NOW!"

Together, the harnessed force of Luminosity fired from Koln and Nischia's connected hands, at the same time as Prisma and Logis. A tremendous wave of glorious Luminosity swept the home up in whole.

Feldra continued to shriek in agony, as she turned to face the group of four, who were impenetrable in their stance. Nischia kept her breath steady as she felt a deep sickness in her stomach. Feldra's face was now going black, like rot in the earth, her mouth drooping, her eyes languid. Her tongue flopped limply out of her mouth, a sickening wet grey, a colour for her corruption.

Words no longer came from her, only spewing, erratic strews of volatile Luminosity. Her eyes seemed to roll back in her head wildly as she let out her assault on her four opponents.

Feldra's darkly hued light collided with their golden wave then, and Nischia felt the force of it as her shoulder popped in response, immediately dislocated. She cried out in pain as her face was slammed by the shockwave, and she fell over, dragging Koln down with her, who landed his full weight upon her limp arm. Nischia felt the crunch of her arm, grinding back into place against the hard ground. Only Prisma and Logis's Luminosity remained now, a steady but weakened flow.

The All-Mother was soaring around the cavern-like home freely within her ring of light. "You will not take them, Feldra," she cautioned loudly. "They are stronger than you. You fade as they go on, and your heart lacks the fullness they share. You will not take these people from me. You will not!" She flared her globe of light suddenly, sucking it into her palms as she dropped from the sky, landing on a shaky leg. The white-hot balls of light danced on the ends of her fingertips, and she flung them at Feldra, who was still distracted by Prisma and Logis's forcefield. The light hit her, splintering her body in several corroded places like dead timber. Bits of Feldra's arms flew off like splinters, her skull breaking open to unveil only specks of glittering dust. The All-Mother's balls of light continued to spread across her body, eating away at it, before finally, her totally decrepit husk of a body was all that remained, shattered across the floor.

"Not all those who are Blessed have the fortitude needed to survive a nova burn. This one was weak of mind and heart, and so she shall never truly rest. The arms of eternity abandon her. Her blackened body will only feed the roots below. Let us cast it out and be done with this evil business. Feldra, once-queen of Adira, is no more!" The All-Mother cried out in pain as soon as she finished her words, stumbling over Feldra's cloven body.

"Mother!" Breaking free of Prisma's grip, Logis ran to the All-Mother, dropping her *cism,* which rolled uselessly along the ground, now devoid of Luminosity entirely.

The All-Mother had collapsed fully now, in the soil of Feldra's dried remains. The black dust that was once a queen coated the All-Mother's aged skin like that of a bruise across her neck and back. She was shaking, her breaths faint. Suddenly, the all-powerful ancient one had become a grey and faded thing to be pitied, a life long-lived slowly terminating before their very eyes. Nischia felt a prick of tears come to her, and she knelt down, not knowing what words she could add that might make things better. Nothing she could do would make it better. It never did. The torment of her failures and the constancy at which they came through her life was inexhaustible, it seemed.

Koln knelt and bowed his head low before the All-Mother, while Logis wept over she who had once given her life in their beautiful home. But now, the room was so cold and desolate, the warmth of the Great Tree's embrace could not be felt. Outside, the sound of fighting continued, the divided people unaware of what had gone on.

As the All-Mother let out her dying breaths, one by one, Nischia counted again.

One. She tried to put an end to her own tears, but to no avail.

Two. Though she wanted to shun the thoughts from her mind, she couldn't help but feel her culpability in the events that had taken place.

Three. Her heart raced with anxiety that set her face to stone, as the heart of the oldest of Aobia's people gave out, and the All-Mother's soul slipped away.

Four. Logis's wails grew louder, a lament that could not be softened. This was grief at its most raw and new. Grief that arrived just as quickly as the All-Mother departed. Nischia swore she could see a tear roll down Koln's cheek, and she heard Prisma sniffling uncontrollably beside her. She had done this. She had been a part of this, again. When would she learn to not hurt those around her?

Five. Nischia was but a child in the eyes of her elders, including both that sat in this room, crying. She looked at the All-Mother, collapsed in a heap on top of Feldra's rot and black dust. *I am just an Aobian with a Blessing,* she heard the dead queen speak, *and with that Blessing comes a duty. An honour. The rest is for the gods.*

An honour, and a duty. And yet here she sat, the reason the greatest of Aobia's lineage was dead, the reason her own queen had been killed. How could she give the rest of her burdens to the gods, the Trees, if she could not handle those immediately set before her?

How could she ever be whole, when she was only becoming more broken, like Feldra's destroyed body, with each new day? The last thing she heard, before they got up to their feet, and treated the dead in the ways they deserved, was her mother's voice.

An insidious curse on our lives.

A curse.

NOW

2055 AS

THE SMELL OF DEATH settled in her nostrils, along with the stiff, clumpy dust of crushed granite and rock. Her eyes would not open, encrusted in the stuff, and she was frigidly cold. From within the rubble, Nischia reached a hand up, peeling away the bits of grit and rock. Eyes now open, she began trying to locate anyone she could from the team. A broken leg, bent backwards and twisted at the kneecap, stuck out of the mess of rocks before her, and she gagged at the sight of it, snapped shin bone torn through skin. Thankfully, it did not belong to one of her own and had crude leather pads on it, as well as the edges of a war-kilt jutting out from the top. She hadn't even considered that Therador's force might have taken a higher path. Sure, it was tighter to navigate, but maybe Cavtil had gotten some of the facts wrong. There was no way they could have marched a small army of two hundred along the clifftops, not without clearing considerable amounts of dense, frozen bush.

She squeezed her way through the debris until she came to a dead end. Voices could be heard from outside, and she prayed silently to the Tree that belonged to her team, but they were muffled. The collapsed rocks here were all loosely put together, their gaps filled with dirt and coarse gravel. She could poke up through it easily enough, but she had no weapons, nothing to keep her protected if she were to appear before the enemy.

She closed her eyes, noticing a faint sound. A pulsing hum was calling to her from back where she'd crawled through, and she knew it was a *cism*. She swung her body around, feeling her robes tear on the jutted ground, rocks grazing her arms and legs. One of her boots was split at the sole and tearing off her foot the more she moved. Eventually she caught the softest glow of the *cism* through a mass of rocks. Grunting, she managed to move some of the bigger ones out of the way because they were so loosely collected.

Nischia found her way around the *cism*, getting enough purchase by lodging herself in an awkward diagonal fashion against some locked-in rocks, so she could spin the glowing orb a little closer to her. With it successfully pulled through the small area she had cleared prior, she got the thing and immediately put her fingertips to it, trying to sense what Luminosity was left within.

She had learned a trick from Koln once, using Luminosity to see heat patterns in the air. If there was enough left within the *cism* she'd retrieved, maybe she could locate the others. Putting her fingertips to the glass sphere, she closed her eyes, trying to take in what little light trickled through her, less like a river before, and more like the slow crawl of honey. She took a deep breath and opened her eyes, sending the Luminosity to them. There was enough. Around her, clusters of red and blue on the air, signalling a mixture of dead bodies and the living. From their outline, she could tell who the Theradorans were, their stocky, human frame barely standing up to the height of an Aobian. Then she whirled her head around as a groan sounded from behind her. An Aobian.

She pulled herself forward on her elbows, using her tattered robes to slide along the ground without cutting herself on the rocks. The *cism* was rocking in her hands, the Luminosity's connection to her body constantly severed and being returned as she tried to stabilise it. She leafed through a thin layer of rock, seeing the outline of the body before, and hearing their panted breaths. "Freya," she muttered. "Freya! It's me, Nischia. Don't move—let me get you out."

"My ... lady," Freya said, her breathing laborious. "My arm, it's stuck. I cannot feel it."

Nischia redirected the flow of the Luminosity to her hands, hoping it would be enough for her to dislodge the large rock that sat directly on Freya's arm, wedged between her wrist and elbow. The fingers were blue—so blue. Nischia bit her lip, trying not to think about it. Perhaps it wasn't too late.

The light allowed her the strength to move the rock, and she slotted it in place beneath a mound of others, all of equal size, to stop the cascading effect of the rocks above. Tugging on Freya's other arm, she dislodged her from the space, pulling her close.

"Freya," she whispered. "You are okay." She felt a lump in her throat. Nobody had told her that as a child, and yet her responsibility was here to fill.

"What of the others?" Freya croaked, coughing lightly, dusty dirt escaping her lungs.

"I cannot make them out from the humans," Nischia said, shaking her head. "In the meantime, let us rise to the surface and see what we are dealing with. Don't speak too loudly. There are voices above us, and I fear they do not belong to our people."

"More of them?" Freya asked in disbelief. "The whole cliff wall came down ... It isn't possible."

"I think there is more to Therador's plans than a simple flanking route, Freya. They took a higher path, which Cavtil was not aware of. What are the chances they didn't also take the one we assumed they would?" She moved away from Freya to a patch of rocks with light jutting in through several cracks. "Here, help me clear this pile. Keep your shoulders and back tense in case you need to carry the weight of any other debris falling as we move it. We need clean air."

AN EERIE CALM SETTLED over the ridge as Prisma approached with a legion of Aobian fighters. The ridge itself was wide, though it sloped down, and the farther along it went, the steeper the decline down the mountainside. It was no place for a battlefield. Beside her, Cavtil grunted as the two fronts pushed towards each other, foreboding step at a time, as though acknowledging this would be their final stand. The nation of Adira would not be long now, she hoped. She'd sent runners to the Peak hours before, when she and Cavtil had heard the sounds of the mountainside crumbling. She'd know. Immediately, something was wrong. If they could hold out against Therador first, the Adiran footmen would be able to mount the clifftops, creating a sense of engulfing from above, swallowing the white land on which they stood.

Though the enemy was not as numerous, Prisma felt her skin crawl at the sight of the man who led them closer and those who surrounded him protectively. Jurin was the emperor-son of Therador, and for his place at the front line, he certainly looked the part. As a younger man, he had seen plenty of bloodshed, having survived the first front at the Outfields of Adira at the age of fifteen. The thing that marked his survival was a hideous tear, a slash of a blade largely unhealed properly, causing his skin to ripple and contort down one side of his face, neck, and onto his chest.

His father, Emperor Holrin, had fought the same war since he became the leader of Therador fifty years ago; it was he who had incited the conflict in the first place, a last-ditch attempt to rectify the divisions among his people at the hand of his own tyrant father. Years of blood, let from the palms of Therador's fathers, had meant the culture of their people was used to, or perhaps even comfortable with violence. They didn't need a force much larger than what they had—the threat they posed here on the mountainside ridge would be enough to change the landscape and perhaps the outcome of the battle that was ongoing up on the Peak.

Around Jurin were an assembly of men dressed in skins, wearing the skulls of their dead over their faces as masks, and cow horns, which had been crudely fused to them.

Priests of Dirt. Prisma had heard of these people, the true leaders of Therador, who spewed their insane doctrines at the civilians and made the nation into the barbaric thing it was today. In Therador, anyone who didn't work was punished with death. If Mother Earth gave people their lives, the least they could do was give all they had back to her.

Prisma scanned the collapsed cliffside, the pile of crushed rock and dirt that had slid down the mountain, a deadly avalanche they had heard back at camp. She hoped that beneath all the debris, someone was alive. And she hoped it was her sister. From behind her, she heard Denlin, the foot commander who had brought the last reserve force they had at the camp, suck in a slow, long breath, as though she was taking air in through a straw. "We wait?" she asked, her voice shaky.

Prisma nodded. "We wait. For the bell to toll, or the horn to sound, or Therador to make their move—we wait."

"What other option do we have?" Cavtil said dismally. He was so small in and amongst the Aobian bodies that were walking with them that Prisma forgot he stood beside her occasionally.

Then, in the dying light of dusk, Prisma saw it. Her first sign of hope. A pale-yellow aura hovered around a collection of rubble, hundreds of feet away. It seemed Jurin and his soldiers had noticed it too. *Sister*, Prisma thought excitedly. *You are alive.*

TOGETHER, THEY MOVED THE rocks, Nischia wincing every time a foreign one struck her in the back as the gap between them increased, eventually allowing her and Freya to crawl through to the open sky. The noise here was ominous and chaotic. Nischia was surprised how much of it had been dampened beneath the surface. All around them stood Theradoran soldiers, who were in formation, watching an opposing force coming from the opposite direction. Daring not to poke her head up beyond the layer of rubble, Nischia peered over the top only to feel the first smile in weeks spread across her face.

"Prisma." She beamed. Her sister for better or for worse, and all she had in this world, had brought the reserve army down the slopes, with none other than Sergeant Cavtil and his Nestler army. Therador were clearly taken aback, roaring aggressively while a group at the front of the lines talked hastily to determine what they should do. Jurin, the heir to Therador, and his Priests of Dirt were exchanging, in heated debate, words to the effect of, "What tipped them off?"

"Come on." Nischia grinned, scooping up Freya by the armpit. "They will not notice us. Let us take them from within."

"Lady Prisma has brought the rest!" Freya cupped a hand to her mouth, shocked.

They stood for a while, in the middle of the debris-strewn snow, looking around at the advancing Theradoran unit, who were sending arrows into the Aobian and Nestler forces beyond, but were not yet moving across the rubble-strewn ground.

"Arondil …" Freya sniffed. "Arondil would have said to act first, not last. I suppose even his fierceness never paid itself back. It's what killed him."

"Never let it be said that fierceness will not yield you the respect you deserve," Nischia said, with a hardness she herself had not anticipated. "Arondil died trying to do the right thing for the rest of us. I have felt what he felt, many times in my life, child. I too, have died out of fierceness, out of want for a better outcome. Sometimes, it simply isn't the way of the gods."

Freya looked at her, incredulous. "You're saying you believe in fate." It was not a question; instead, it was a disappointment.

"I'm saying all we can do is our duty," Nischia murmured, feeling the *cism* that was tucked within her robes. She gritted her teeth, watching Jurin raise his sword to the sky, the rear artillery lines of the Theradoran army raising their bows with him. "As long as we do that, the rest, we must leave to them. The Trees are with us, child. They run in our very blood, even the ones we no longer reside in. Let them guide you and *be fierce*."

She steeled herself to the rising drones of the warhorns, all around her, as the Theradoran army let their first arrows loose, and the front lines charged at one another. "Stay behind them Freya, and be as steel. Slay who you can, and leave none to rest, unless it is with their bones."

PRISMA AND CAVTIL STOOD, back-to-back, swirling around as Theradoran soldiers tried to strike them down, running through their first line and into the army behind them, crushing soldiers as a result of the smallest errors, or strokes of poor luck. Careful not to trip over larger pieces of rubble that lay across the snowy ground, Prisma kept her *cism* activated in one hand, a shield in her other. She pushed all the light she could into her shield hand, and rammed any enemy who came close.

"Cavtil!" she cried over the sound of blades and death. "Their force is larger than ours—there are still some above us, on the cliffs!"

Cavtil's only response was to curse loudly, before sticking an enemy's belly with his spear, ripping it free with a grunt. They had evaded the first set of attackers and would need to try and push forward into the Theradoran army where Jurin and his Priests were. Right as they began their charge through the snow, the lobbing volley of flaming arrows overhead began, like the snow itself was on fire. The gale scooped up some of them, sending their flames into winter-dry trees and dead branches, kicking up small spot-fires all over the ridge.

"The fire will block our lines, Cavtil!" Prisma yelled.

"Run through!" the sergeant replied. "Do not stop. There are enough feet to trample the fire out as we cross."

Prisma felt her heart in her temples. The light in her *cism* was running out, and she feared she was not strong enough to make an impact with her shield without the influence of Luminosity. She glanced at the ridge, sloping downwards beyond the Theradorans, and gasped. Pikes rose from behind the enemy forces. There were more. If the ally armies didn't have men on the ground coming to fight with them, this would truly be Aobia's last stand, and the Mountain Pass would undoubtedly become Therador's.

Cavtil smacked a Theradoran right in the crotch of his kilt before registering the same thing Prisma noticed. His little eyes seemed to swell in fear. Then, his face changed for the better, and he leapt for joy, his furry ears dancing upon his head. "Adira! The allies come!" Turning to face his army, he gave the command: "CHARGE!"

NISCHIA DREW FROM THE *cism* again while Freya defended her with a short knife. Directing all the Luminosity to her eyes again, Nischia looked frantically around for anyone else who might have escaped the avalanche. She saw one body, its outline a cooler purple than red, and surged forward.

"Freya! There's one over here!"

Freya kept her closely guarded, and they leapt together, until they were down beside the body.

"Roots below," Nischia swore under her breath.

They sat behind a short cleft of hill, suddenly out of sight of the enemy. The body beside them belonged to quiet Hadi. Nischia didn't think it possible for him to be any quieter than he already was, but the lack of breath moving through his lungs told it all.

Freya glanced at Hadi's body sadly, her bottom lip quivering. "How many did we lose in that collapse?"

Nischia didn't say a word. She had brought the mountainside crashing down. Maybe it was a valiant attempt to quell the Theradoran suppressors above them, but the spiralling effects of her actions continued to haunt her. She flinched as a hand touched her shoulder, before jumping backward in fright when she realised it did not belong to Freya.

"Lady Nischia."

Valton, Gest, and the Nestlers stood before her, right next to a fallen tree. They must have been there the entire time, and she hadn't seen them. She could have cried with joy to see them, a reminder that not all she did was detrimental to those around her.

Freya filled the intermittent silence with tears for her, and she let out a relieved sigh. "You all made it," she said, smiling. Valton's face fell, however, as his twin sister spoke for him.

"Wes did not make it," she said, clearing her throat. "We couldn't retrieve ... all of him." She handed a silver brooch to Freya, and for a moment, the sounds of battle behind them all faded away. Freya's tears stopped, and she pressed the cold metal to her cheek. "Roots take you, Wes."

"Garv does not wish to ... dismantle the moment," the small commander said, "but we are needed. Take up whatever you have and fight. We managed to preserve this, in all the chaos." Walking around the back of the fallen tree, Garv and the other Nestlers revealed the supply trailer that should have been completely destroyed in the fall. Despite her disbelief, Nischia could only feel gratitude for the small Nestlers, and she drew back the cover on top of the trailer eagerly. Four *cism,* all completely intact, several sheathless blades, and a shortened quill of arrows.

As the team drew out the supplies they needed, warhorns sounded, a different tone to that of the Theradorans, who had now met with Aobia on the ridge. Nischia caught the wave of pikes racing up the hill, and the light green leather of Adiran soldiers. "Adira, on the ridge. Look!" Riding at the frontlines was the familiar, blonde haired, blue-eyed boy she'd seen fifty years ago, now in the later years of his life. King Filens, accompanied by his son, the young heir Terrens. There was no reason for the king himself to be here, on the mountain, while the fighting went on outside Adira as well. She peered in his direction intently, wondering why he was a part of this skirmish, beneath the peak of the mountain.

The team then ran forward with the Adiran lines, and Nischia pressed two *cism* together in an attempt to harness twice the amount of Luminosity, something which Koln had warned her against as a learning Sleeper. In the heat of battle, however, she knew what she needed to do. She let out a burst of light in the faces of the Theradorans who had turned around to engage with Adira, blinding them instantly, sending some spinning, disoriented completely.

The Adiran lines, however, did not strike a blow. In fact, they stopped short, cutting her momentum off entirely. They continued blowing their horns and divided into two rows, allowing their king and prince to ride between them, to the top of the next hill on the ridge, where the bulk of the fighting was taking place. The resounding dissonance of the horns rose in a swelling crescendo, slowly stifling the fighting to null. The Aobian and Theradoran armies looked to the king with a mixture of curiosity and irritation. Then the words came, the words that would define a generation of humans, and mark a change in the course of Q'ara's history.

"Place down your weapons, men of Adira, tree-dwellers of Aobia, Hidden People, and Therador. The Four-Front War is over," began Filens in a low, resonant voice. "The Armistice has been signed one week past, the fighting on the Adiran Outfields finished. The treaties have been exchanged, and the time of peace on this land begins now!" With a roar of passion, the king swung his mighty sword over his head, the rest of the Adiran army matching his energy, as the battlefield diffused. Nischia stood, unwavering, uncertain of what had happened, while the Nestlers embraced on one side of her and her team of Aobians on the other.

The war was over. Fifty years of conflict. From the moment Feldra's death became public across the continent, until now, needless blood had been shed in Adira, Therador, Ghabbat, and the Mountain. Now, they could all go home. They could celebrate with their friends, and embrace their families.

They could rest.

THEN

1958 AS

THE CITY OF ADIRA, the Sea Kingdom, was a marvel of human design and art making, a perfect blend of smooth architecture, symmetrical lines, and curves. Huge, white, sandstone walls shaped its three districts all around the Palace, which was set into the city's rear, and partly exposed to the wide beaches of pure sand, and aqua blue waters. It nearly provided the relief Nischia needed, to move past the pain of Feldra's death, which was now her duty to share with the human king, a young man of eighteen, no more, named Filens.

Koln had remained in Aobia, as was custom for all Aobians; only ambassadors were cleared for such travel. This, however, was a very rare exception, and Nischia was acutely aware of the weight of it. She had been one of a few to witness Feldra's state of decay, and her exile at the hands of the All-Mother. Logis had taken the dead queen then, and disposed of her.

Feldra's sentence was no easy fate, and yet it happened as swiftly as anything. Standing atop the highest limb of the Mind, she took a step out into the great beyond and fell through an invisible wall of her mistakes, her grieving people, and her ultimate end. Whether she survived the fall or not did not matter.

The monarchy had ended, and the Magisterium led the way now, a new nation carved out of its ancient ashes. There were to be significant social reforms, such as the formal banning of Naming rituals, and the free education the new republic would offer to its young.

The new All-Mother had receded afterwards, into her branch-home, to quietly grieve her own mother. Enclosed in there once more, she entrusted her people to Staril and her government, before emerging to announce that she would be the one to accompany Nischia to Adira, and she had another purpose altogether. She was to be taken under the employ of the new king to head a research team. Nischia was surprised that this had been approved by the Magisterium, but then again, who were they to question the last in Tala's line, the original steward of the Aobian people, who had rescued them from nomadism and brought them to their first Tree? When Logis's mother died, she had become the All-Mother, but she had made it explicitly clear she had no interest in assuming that role for Aobia. For the republic to succeed, she'd told Nischia during their travels, they would have to shirk every deeply rooted tradition they could, because many times, deeply rooted traditions held no relevance in meaning to a modern age. Nischia found it hard to decide whether or not she agreed, given the recent events.

The journey through the three districts of Adira would take no more than two hours by caravan, and just like the rest of Q'ara that Nischia had been privileged enough to see, her eyes were filled with wonder. But she was a realist, and she knew nothing of these people's lives compared with what she had under the safe embrace of the Great Tree. Despite Logis saying the contrary, Nischia felt the Tree calling to her at the oddest times when they'd first set out for Adira. It wasn't until they crossed the Mountain Pass, which lay between the nations of Therador, Adira, and Aobia, that she truly felt the desolation of being away from home, a collection of loneliness and aloneness all at once.

These streets were beautiful, but they were not the same. The first district was a mixture of residential living and open markets that stretched out all the way around the city, terminating at the beautiful white-sand beaches. Life bubbled away in it, though it lacked the vigour and passion of the creative minds who lived and worked in The Soul. The second was cleaner and more refined, as well as being perhaps the epitome of a visitor's experience of the kingdom. The white stone walls were kept clean, and the effects of the saltwater sea seemed not to have any effect on the buildings.

What was truly staggering, however, was the beginning of the third district. Each of the districts were marked by gargantuan metal gates, cut into ornate shapes and patterns, and highly secured with both a lever and a bar lock. But the third district was distinct because it marked the entrance to the enormous Palace that scaled the inclining hills of Adira, sitting above the city like a beacon, and spreading across to the sea. The gate that marked its entrance was kept open much of the time by contrast to the others, and it was filled with deckled glass, allowing the sunlight to find its way through on magical angles. Right beyond the gate was a glass-domed area that reached up enough to nearly touch the sky when one stood beneath it. When they stepped inside the massive lobby, they were well met by a party of guards, with the king himself in tow.

Filens was a sight to behold for a human, and Nischia felt her eyes stay on him longer than was comfortable. He had a well-chiselled jaw and long locks of blond hair. He was larger than life too, dwarfing many of his guards, but it was clear he was human, and he stood a head shorter than Nischia, Logis, and the accompanying ambassadors, Agnar and Zayna.

"Revered tree-dwellers," the king announced in a grand voice, rich like honey. "Welcome to Adira, the Sea Kingdom."

"Your Majesty," Nischia bowed her head with the other three, kneeling down.

"Do not kneel for me, stewards of Q'ara," Filens said with an endearing smile. "I am not worthy of such reverence." These words struck a deep part of Nischia's heart, and she felt a profound respect for the young king. Though she and the other three Aobians had been treated with respect in every town they visited after leaving the Tree, not once could she recall a time that a human had acknowledged them for what they were: the original custodians of this land, Q'ara. The bloodlines of Aobia had mixed for centuries, and in Ghabbat, for instance, a northern nation on the continent, the original Aobians were nowhere to be seen, having bred for generations with the humans that settled there. They were distant relatives of Nischia's kind anyway, the true Aobians who shared a unique relationship with the Great Tree. "I am graced with your presence," the king went on. "But I know you do not come before me with the same pleasure."

"We do not," Logis said in her old and husky voice. "But never has pleasure replaced necessity, O King of the Sea."

Filens nodded. "Then let us come together for a meal in my garden and talk about all that must be talked about. I will not keep you here longer than your heart can take. I am not an unkind king."

THEY SAT IN THE king's splendid gardens, overlooking the calm, blue sea. The majesty of Adira in the summertime was nothing to scoff at, and even Nischia felt drawn by the idea of extending her stay. She had no doubt that Logis would not need to reconsider her offer now they were here. They ate freshly cured olives, with dabs of goat's cheese, smeared onto warm pieces of flatbread. They drank the wine of the Adiran vineyards, which ran across the northern hills beyond the city. Before the talking began, the illusion that all was good in the world perforated Nischia's reality.

"I am prepared to receive whatever news you have for me, tree-dwellers. It is a momentous occasion to be visited by two Sleepers of the Great Tree. I believe even my father before me was not granted the privilege." Filens crossed his arms after sipping from his wine glass.

"Truly, Your Majesty, we have no good news to give." Logis looked down at the table. "But we must give it to you regardless. Nischia?" Her eyes had lost the shine that Nischia had seen in them the first time she'd met Logis, in the branch-home. Nischia knew the older Sleeper had thoughts only for her mother.

"Y—Your Majesty," Nischia said, stuttering nervously. "Two weeks ago, we set off from Aobia in the wake of the most turbulent of times. It was the fastest and gravest of days that ended that week, and our nation has changed forever. For the better, we hope."

Filens raised an eyebrow, glancing at both Agnar and Zayna. "You do not envy these guests for telling me this tragic story." Agnar shook his head, and Zayna simply sighed as she went back to her wine. The King continued. "I fear I know where this story is going. Before you go on, Lady Sleeper, just know that the corrupt treasurer responsible for illegal dealings with Aobia has been dismissed from duty and imprisoned."

"I understand," Logis said. "Queen Feldra is dead, and I cannot sit on the matter any other way. It must be said as plainly as that. My mother before me was one of the Ancients, the second generation to have lived in our Great Tree. It was she who died at the queen's hands, and she who also freed my people from Feldra's tyranny."

"Tyranny?" Filens stroked his stubbly chin. "Hm ... Agnar, this came back to me quicker than I expected."

Agnar let out a hard breath. "Yes, Your Majesty. It seems that within hours of the announcement that Feldra had shared *cism* with Adiran and Theradoran underground members, the streets were a battlefield. The queen supercharged her Luminosity to escape from a contained prison cell before leading a small unit of sympathisers in a bloodbath. The Tree has changed forever, sire. Feldra was outnumbered."

Filens remained quiet, but his face did not waver. He sat back, letting the hot afternoon sun drape him.

Nischia picked up where Agnar had finished. "I can't say I am surprised now that we know the depths of her crime. Your Majesty, as of three weeks ago, Aobia became a republic, free of the shackles of the monarchy."

Filens leaned forward in his seat, covering his now sweaty forehead with one hand. "A republic," he muttered. Nischia looked to Logis expectantly.

"My people are better for it, King of Adira. Years have passed where we have wanted change. You may not have been privy to this ... slow turn in our culture."

"Better for it?" A hint of anger touched King Filens's voice. It wasn't his country. Why did he carry such heat in his words? "What makes it better, to abandon your leader? One rotten egg amongst a dozen does not undo the rest."

Nischia shifted uncomfortably. "There are traditions our people held onto for no want of their own, King Filens. Abhorrent Naming rituals, manipulative Luminosity…our people have been prisoners for centuries, without suspecting a thing."

"I've heard of these Naming rituals." Filens cracked his knuckles, an unseemly action for a king. "You can assure me then that these have been outlawed?"

"Nothing pleases me more greatly than the outlaw of Naming rituals, sire," Logis said. "The people will be free now, free to choose what they wish."

"Your people have an ingrained mindset, child of the All-Mother." Filens did not know his title for Logis was inaccurate, but Nischia caught a slight furrow on Logis's brow as he said the words. *She* was the All-Mother now, and the fact of it made her decision to leave all the more difficult. "I fear you will not escape it, despite your attempts to quell these antiquities behaviours."

"We are not monsters, Your Majesty, and I suggest you do not overextend your words." Logis gritted her teeth. Nischia squeezed her shoulders together, an attempt to diffuse the tension within her. From now on, she would have to let Logis lead, for fear of slipping her tongue. The human king had an allure to him that was both disconcerting as much as it was precarious.

"I apologise, child of the All-Mother. I did not intend offence. Tradition holds with it certain dangers, as it does parameters for celebration of a culture. It is everything you are, and everything you might not want to be."

"You make it sound as though tradition and identity are synonymous," Nischia interjected with a grimace. She had walked the path of tradition, and still she knew nothing of who she was.

"I merely point out, Lady Sleeper, that our traditions must be subjected to change. Your people have a rich history on the earth, written into the very veins of Q'ara itself, unlike my own. Finding a balance between the things that make good on that history, and those you must let go of is not an enviable task." Filens sighed. "I'm sorry to hear of the end the queen met. I had met her in person only once, as a young child. Forgive me if I do not seem upset, to the proper degree. May your people find peace." He stood up, gesturing to the table. "I will leave you here to enjoy this afternoon tea, and we can talk more officially with the council at dinner. I judge that the love of friends still exists between our two great nations?"

"Of course," Logis said. With a look at Nischia that could only be foreshadowing, she too stood up. "Your Majesty, might I have a private word with you, before we go?"

Filens nodded, and they stepped back into the Palace through a wide, double-doored entry. Nischia could only hear the muffled tones of voices from behind the glass panels, but she knew what it was. Logis had lost her home, and her heart. Perhaps those two things were the same. Though they would be shorter in number than the rest of her people in the Tree, she could live out her days, beyond the reach of the Tree, and be joyous here. Maybe not happy, but joyous.

Nischia tugged subconsciously at her hair, twisting it around her fingers, and looking at it, still glowing somewhat despite the rich sunlight striking down on her from above. A glow that ran through her, a symbol of what she'd become. She was no demi-god, like the common folk pretended she was. And what she'd become was not consistent with who she thought she used to be.

Home, and heart. Both were things she did not have. She glanced around the white stone walls. They were as alien to her as her own hair.

Eventually, she went inside to rest in a big, luxurious room she could have all to herself, until it was time to return to the Tree. A place she was obligated to return. In the quiet of the darkening day, edging closer towards the late evening of the summer, Nischia cried herself to sleep in a bed for kings and queens, alone. Abandoned.

Unbelonging.

THE END OF

THE REST TO THE GODS

A QUICK WORD...

So, you've made it this far. Thanks for reading *The Rest to the Gods*! This one has been a lot of fun to write, and I can't wait to show you all more the continent Q'ara. To stay up to date with me and my work, check out my mailing list at: www.joshuawalkerauthor.com/subscribe

Nothing fulfils me more than getting my work into the hands of readers. If you wouldn't mind leaving me a review on Goodreads and Amazon, (or if you can't, a star rating would also be fabulous), I can do exactly that.

In the current state of publishing, a review goes a long way to getting my writing out there and in front of more readers!

Josh
January 2024

ACKNOWLEDGEMENTS

There is nothing about this book that is small besides its page count, and I really mean that. From the bottom of my heart, I am deeply thankful to every person who got this novella to where I hoped it would be when I first drafted it.

But before I even get to the people who directly shaped this story, I need to start at the very beginning.

To my Creator, without which I would not have been blessed with these talents. What more can I say than that?

To my parents and brothers, who all played a part in my love of stories over the years, thank you. From the moment I read The Hobbit, to tearing through Dad's white cupboard filled with Marvel and DC hits, to sabotaging my grandparents' computer to write some pretty bad attempts at stories instead of playing video games, I was set upon this path. I believe this to be just the beginning in what will hopefully eventuate in a momentous career as an author.

To my wife for being unceasingly supportive of me hiding in "the cave," thank you. I love you and could not do any of this without you.

To my best friends, Sam and Christian, who put up with my crap, read my other crap, and try to polish the crap into a lovely looking crap that I can actually do something with—you guys inspire me and always encourage me to keep going. I hope I do the same for you.

Onto the team that got this story to where it is, and I cannot start without mentioning my author's group, The Break-Ins. Scott Palmer, who set the group up with me back in October of this year, along with

Rob Leigh, Isaac Hill, Kaden Love, Adrian M Gibson, Louise Holland, and Calum Lott—you all *rock*.

My beta readers set the foundations for my editor to do her best. Thank you to Joe, Alex, Isaac, Scott, and Calum.

To my editor Belle for being super perfunctory and providing only the best constructive criticisms, as well as my proofreader Rachel for her keen eye on my excessive comma usage—thank you so much.

To everyone in the indie community who has been helpful and lovely from the moment we first spoke: I will work to repay each and every one of you for taking a chance on me. There are so many people I have interacted with that I can't possibly list here, but just know I appreciate you all.

To my brilliant cover designer, Stef: it has been a pleasure to work with you, and I honestly can't wait to chat all things Novella #2 when the time comes. If anyone needs amazing cover art, Seventhstar Art Services is the place to go!

Lastly, to you, dear reader. Nothing matters if there isn't a soul to enjoy these stories. I will keep writing for as long as I can, as long as you keep reading, keep imagining, and keep dreaming. There are worlds out there for all of us to explore, and this is only one of them.

ABOUT THE AUTHOR

Joshua Walker is a fantasy author from Melbourne, Australia. He currently works as a primary school English teacher, and likes to read, brew beer, and hang out with his wife and BFD (Big Fluffy Dog), Otis, in his free time.

To find out more about The Song of the Sleepers series, go to www.joshuawalkerauthor.com.